Young Writers 2005 CREATIVE WRITING
COMPETITION FOR SECONDARY SCHOOLS

T·A·L·E·S·

From South East England
Vol II
Edited by Bobby Tobolik

Disclaimer

Young Writers has maintained every effort
to publish stories that will not cause offence.

Any stories, events or activities relating to individuals
should be read as fictional pieces and not construed
as real-life character portrayal.

Young Writers

First published in Great Britain in 2005 by:
Young Writers
Remus House
Coltsfoot Drive
Peterborough
PE2 9JX
Telephone: 01733 890066
Website: www.youngwriters.co.uk

All Rights Reserved

© Copyright Contributors 2005

SB ISBN 1 84602 278 9

Foreword

Young Writers was established in 1991 and has been passionately devoted to the promotion of reading and writing in children and young adults ever since. The quest continues today. *Young Writers* remains as committed to engendering the fostering of burgeoning poetic and literary talent as ever.

This year, *Young Writers* are happy to present a dynamic and entertaining new selection of the best creative writing from a talented and diverse cross section of some of the most accomplished secondary school writers around. Entrants were presented with four inspirational and challenging themes.

'Myths And Legends' gave pupils the opportunity to adapt long-established tales from mythology (whether Greek, Roman, Arthurian or more conventional eg The Loch Ness monster) to their own style.

'A Day In The Life Of ...' offered pupils the chance to depict twenty-four hours in the lives of literally anyone they could imagine. A hugely imaginative wealth of entries were received encompassing days in the lives of everyone from the top media celebrities to historical figures like Henry VIII or a typical soldier from the First World War.

Finally 'Short Stories', in contrast, offered no limit other than the author's own imagination while 'Hold The Front Page' provided the ideal opportunity to challenge the entrants' journalistic skills, asking them to provide a newspaper or magazine article on any subject of their choice.

T.A.L.E.S. From South East England Vol II is ultimately a collection we feel sure you will love, featuring as it does the work of the best young authors writing today.

Contents

Bradfield College, Reading
Thomas Pinder (13)	1
Peter Rakic (15)	2
Hattie Pearson (15)	3
Thomas Arnold (14)	4
James Shields (14)	5
Michael Digby (14)	6
James Peet (14)	7
Alicia Lindsay (18)	8
Stefan F Heffron (14)	10

Cardinal Wiseman RC High School, Greenford
Sayo Addous (13)	11
Erika Scarth (13)	12
Lydia Shellien-Walker (15)	13
Zoë Plant (15)	14

Kennet School, Thatcham
Mark Conway (14)	16
Stephanie Marshall (15)	17
Shaun Martin (15)	18
Elouise Field (12)	19
Trudi Hanson (13)	20
Samantha Friday (14)	21

Langleywood School, Slough
Kimberley Buckland (14)	22
Tenisha Trotman (14)	23
Sabrina Spicer (14)	24
Lynsey Johnston (14)	25
Jamie Whittington (13)	26
Amunpreet Bains (14)	27
Daniel Keates (13)	28
Sunil Ram (14)	29
Mark Taylor (14)	30

Matthew Arnold School, Oxford

Michael Hooton (14)	31
Jamie Cummings (14)	32
Michael Hodges (14)	33
Alex Gibson (14)	34
Bryony Rose (11)	35
Spencer Ramsay (12)	36
Greg Terry (12)	37
Emma Livett (13)	38
Thomas Connick (13)	39
David Owen (12)	40
Stephanie Mileson (12)	42
Hayley Trendell (14)	43
Riziki Summers (14)	44
Sophie Cook (12)	45
Freya Bower (11)	46
David McIver (12)	47
Kiranjit Kamal (12)	48
Ben Hackett (12)	49
Shannen Bound (12)	50
Jessica Ballard (12)	51
Joe Jenkins (14)	52
Robert Whitelock (13)	53
Jack Leahy (13)	54
Phillipa Franklin (12)	55
Danielle Warren (13)	56
Ahsan Hussain (14)	57
Jamie Cole (13)	58
Jonnelle Jones (14)	59
Rosie Kirkbride (14)	60
Sadiya Bi (14)	61
Joe Harrison (12)	62
Michael Younie (12)	63
Josh Thorpe (13)	64
Christina Simeone (13)	65
Jack Preston (13)	66
Sophie Hutton (12)	67
Cathy Van Hear (12)	68
Hannah Robson (12)	69
Sarah Montgomery (11)	70
Jenny Crosby (12)	71

Tessa Hughes (12)	72
Maariyah Razaq (14)	73
Hadia Mansour (13)	74
Tobias Warwick (13)	75
Edmund O'Malley (12)	76
Alicia Hulewicz (11)	77
George Newson (13)	78
Aiya Jibali (13)	79
Tom Peacock (13)	80
Sabrina Gardner (13)	81
Max Bolton (14)	82
Elizabeth Webb (14)	83
James Dallimore (13)	84
Gary Rawlings (12)	85
Amy Grant (12)	86
Oliver Crosbie-Higgs (12)	87
Olivia Sharp (12)	88
James Logan (12)	89
Kieran Tiller (14)	90
Adil Hussain (13)	91
Samantha Hobbs (14)	92
Ashley Creed (14)	93
Robert Tyreman (13)	94
Polly Dunsmore (12)	95
Georgia Fogden (12)	96
Rachel Gibbs (13)	97
James Walsh (13)	98
James Kaye (13)	99
Martha Howells (13)	100
Nicholas Salmon (13)	101
Robert Hainge (13)	102
Sam Trinder (12)	103
Lauren Gayton (11)	104
Peter Endicott (12)	105
Robin Smith (11)	106
Daniel Saxton (12)	107
Kelly Kochanski (11)	108
Mike Whillock (12)	109
James Bedingham (13)	110
Ellie Smith (14)	111
Joshua McCaffer (12)	112
Lewis Knox (11)	113

Sam Matthews (14) — 114
Christopher Benton (14) — 115
Harvey Frost (12) — 116
James Little (12) — 117
Bethany Winch (12) — 118
Georgie Wines (12) — 119
Bianca Donnelly (12) — 120
Sophie Gower (14) — 121
Craig Skinner (14) — 122
Gemma-Whitney Chobbah (13) — 123
Sam Byrne (14) — 124
Iona Sinclair (13) — 125
Conor Merritt (13) — 126
Charlotte Jeffries (12) — 127
Thomas Joyce (13) — 128
Jack Parry (11) — 129
Luke Botham (12) — 130
Eleanor Ewers (12) — 131
Sam Higgs (13) — 132
Connor Blakey (12) — 134
Joshua Bourton (13) — 135
Rose Friedland (13) — 136
Melissa Mulvany (13) — 137
Jess Logan (12) — 138
Hannah Pye (13) — 139
Josie Pye (13) — 140
Michael Njuguna (13) — 141
Josh Kenyon (13) — 142
Jenny Briggs (12) — 143
Sarah Foster (12) — 144
Jess Beasley (13) — 145
Adam Felix (13) — 146
Daniel Pickard (13) — 147
Ryan Smith (12) — 148
Ryan Louise (13) — 149

St Martin's School, Northwood
Shan Ahluwalia (13) — 150
Rohan Dey (12) — 151
Jonathan Barker (13) — 152
Shabbir Merali (13) — 153

Mohsin Saleh (12)	154
Alex Freethy (13)	155
Nikhil Patel (11)	156
Charles Constable (11)	157
Samuel Klein (13)	158
Yuki Yoshimura (12)	159
Azaan Mohamed (11)	160
Hasaan Ausat (12)	161
George Clark (12)	162
Alex Cockerham (11)	163
Elliott Edwards (13)	164
Nikhil Patel (13)	165
Greg Zimmerman (12)	166
Richard Gallagher (12)	167
Hamza Sheikh (12)	168
Sajan Shah (13)	169
William Pithers (11)	170
Christian Shephard (12)	171
Romin Mukadam (12)	172
Daniel Edward (12)	173
Zaid Hamid (11)	174
Sachin Hoyle (12)	175
Leo Pascoulis (12)	176
James Elliott-Vincent (13)	177
Oliver Bello (13)	178
Tom Westford (11)	179
Vincent Moses (13)	180
Mobeen Syed (12)	181
Aramide Oladipo (13)	182
Shivum Taank (13)	183
Himesh Naik (12)	184
Farhan Zubair (13)	185
Il-Kweon Sir (11)	186
Rajiv Kotecha (13)	187
Aaron Ashby-Gittins (12)	188
Krisant Valentine (12)	189
Thomas Minihan (12)	190
Reuben Green (12)	191
Stephen Kemp (11)	192
Shaneel Shah (11)	193
Breman Rajkumar (13)	194
Nikesh Arya (11)	195

Paras Shah (12) 196
Sachin Majithia (13) 197
Patrick Wray (11) 198
Nicholas Tidmarsh (12) 199
Arjun Nijher (12) 200

Waldegrave School for Girls, Twickenham
Abigail Kipps (12) 201
Sophie Alys Hopkins (12) 202
Rosie Parr (12) 203
Tiffany May Pope (11) 204
Lauren Yerby (12) 205
Iva Visnjevac (12) 206
Catherine Bell (12) 208
Abigail Lyons (11) 209
Grace Verghis (11) 210
Amy Hemsley (11) 211
Catherine Ollington (12) 212
Emilie Ruddick (12) 214
Henna Lakha (12) 215
Amy Barnett (12) 216
Stephanie Marquardt (11) 217
Imogen Mathews (12) 218
Taylor Rowe (12) 219
Hattie Morgan (12) 220
Katie Zgorska (12) 221
Aziza Khanom (12) 222
Suzie Harrison (12) 223
Ilana Blum (11) 224
Sophie Wilson (12) 226
Sashka Young (12) 227
Catherine Hale (12) 228
Neetu Dhillon (12) 229
Francesca Twynam (11) 230
Rachel Budden (12) 231
Jessica Wolf (11) 232

The Creative Writing

A Gothic Approach

Darkness fell, it was 18.20. I jumped off the tube with all my bags, they were heavy, too heavy. No one else got off with me, a chilling wind bit at the parts of my body that were not protected by my school sports clothes. I walked down the platform and put my ticket, which I couldn't locate at first, through the machine and the doors opened and I was free again. I could walk home now, to my nice, cosy home, where my family would be. A few cars passed me and beeped their horns as I tried to cross the road. Street lights fluttered about in the dark and shops began to close. There was no one and it was 18.30, how odd and peculiar. I had never seen this before.

I walked further and further, trudging along with my bags, which now seemed like a punishment of weights around my neck. I was walking into the unknown. I reached the park gates, they were open, that was odd again, they normally shut when light disappeared from the cold sky. Now normally I would not walk through these 'forbidden' woods because my friends would tell me not to. But with horrific weights on my shoulders and with me wanting to get home as soon as possible, I walked through and little did I know what I would encounter.

Trees looked at me, birds squawked at me, 'Get out, *get out.*' Squirrels rustled in the bushes, and what horrified me most was the laughing of people in bushes that seemed invisible to me in this light. The path became a mudbath and my white shoes were a hideous shade of murky brown. I began to run and stumble about, trying to get out of this prison.

I saw lights and I saw people walking on the street. I ran out but there was one thing stopping me, the gates had been locked and I was now trapped in this horror. I remembered as a little child being stuck in the park, but it was a lovely summer evening and I was with my mum, dad and sisters. We simply called for the man who lived in the house by the park gates and he let us out. But now I called, and there was no reply. I had to stay the night in this gothic nightmare.

Thomas Pinder (13)
Bradfield College, Reading

The Living Plains

Whiteness was everywhere, shiny bright rays flew in every direction and some undetermined force was strengthening me. I felt free and fresh. I was happy, not one bad memory ever lay in my spiritual mind. I laid flat on some green grass and I heard the trickle of splashing water in the background. I had a clear conscience and I felt like I would be happy forever.

I was so tranced into being someone that in my world never existed. I was utterly full of deep and emotional feelings, like nothing in the world mattered. I hadn't even recollected how and why I was there. I was too bewildered by the God-like world. I slowly opened my eyes effortlessly as I lay on the grass without force. I looked into the clear and sunny sky; it was so beautiful, no words could describe such purity.

I slowly got up and I felt like there were no gravity. My muscles weren't straining. It seemed that I couldn't feel any of my muscles, yet it got up with ease. I didn't feel any pressure on my feet as I stood up, it was as if I were hovering over the floor. I started to glide whilst glaring at the incredible forest that surrounded me. I heard colourful and dashing birds singing, perched on the treetops. I glided across the clean grass. I saw on my left someone that shocked me, this person was Roger! He was alive!

Peter Rakic (15)
Bradfield College, Reading

A Day In My Life In 15 Years' Time

I awoke that frosty morning to the sound of the phone violently screaming at me to pick up. Probably just Mum I assumed, wondering how the promotion party went last night at the office. She cared about me a lot and I really appreciated that, after all, I wouldn't be where I am now if it wasn't for everything she had done for me.

As the phone rang my heart pounded faster and faster as I hoped that it could just possibly be Jake, a tall, dark, handsome creature, the 'Prince Charming' every woman dreamed for. Jake worked on the third floor. I often made petty excuses to go up and strut past his desk, hoping he would notice me. The excuse I often used was that the photocopier on my floor was broken, which never really worked, considering there were actually three on the floor. 'How can all three photocopiers be broken?' asked my boss.

I just wanted to see his cute smile and hear his deep husky voice ricochet off the walls of the busy office. He had even winked at me once or twice - sad I know, *but that must mean something,* I thought to myself as I sat at my desk doodling on a scrap piece of paper in daydream on a quiet summer afternoon in the office. I have the feelings for him, like a teenager would have over their first crush at secondary school.

Hattie Pearson (15)
Bradfield College, Reading

Myths And Legends

Hi, I'm Phillipus, and this is my story.

It happened 3 days ago. I had just finished my work for that tiring day, I was exorcised. I'm a priest. I work in Zeus' temple. It's a beautiful place, full of gold and foreign riches, it's a nice place to work in.

It was this night when it happened. All the other priests had finished their work and were probably all asleep. My job is to look after all the temple's books and notes. I don't know why I was given this job, as I have reading difficulties.

Anyway, I walked slowly into the main temple, so that I could make as little noise as possible, this was where the grand gold statue of the almighty Zeus was sitting on his ivory and silver plated throne. Suddenly I heard a man speaking. I was quiet and stayed behind a pillar. At first I thought he was speaking to me, but as I poked my head around the corner, I saw that this young lad was speaking to the statue - the statue of Zeus.

Without any warning the roof split into two and from this opening came the most beautiful horse I have ever seen. It was not any horse, it had wings. I heard the man call it Pegasus. Pegasus' hair was silver; it glistened in the moonlight and this is what has changed my view on the beauty of life forever.

Thomas Arnold (14)
Bradfield College, Reading

Odysseus '05

We had been travelling for ages. The M4 was blocked and had been diverted, we were unsure of our location. The direction signs gradually stopped and as the light descended, so too the amount of cars accompanying us.

We were all frustrated as we had been away from home for over 10 weeks and needed a rest. As we travelled the visibility got bad, the lack of working road lights prevented us from moving quickly. We grew impatient and tired, desperate for a break. Our standards of living lowered until we saw a sign for a bed and breakfast. With anticipation we decided to go for it.

Upon arriving we saw the seedy old building, not as promising as its lovely sign post.

We entered the open door. The house was single roomed but still filled with anything we would wish for. So hungry we were we helped ourselves to everything we could see including the large volume of beer - we sadly got a bit drunk.

The morning came. It seemed like two of my crew were missing and we searched but with no luck. We saw dark red blood dripping in the direction of the stairs ...

James Shields (14)
Bradfield College, Reading

Skylla And Charybdis

Odysseus and his men had sailed past the sirens. Odysseus tied himself down so he would not be killed by them. As they sailed down another path Odysseus knew that they were going towards Skylla and Charybdis. However, there was no other path to take. He had heard about them from sailors in the past. Skylla was a huge monstrous creature. She was 12 feet tall. Not only that, but she had 6 heads, each had 3 rows of teeth. She lived in a cave on the edge of a cliff. When ships sailed past she snatched them and ate them alive.

Charybdis was a huge whirlpool. It had no body, just a huge mouth. When ships sailed over it, it opened up its mouth and drunk everyone and everything around her.

As Odysseus sailed closer they saw the huge boiling whirlpool up ahead of them. However, it was too late, she had already opened her jaws. Odysseus' men rowed hard to the right, they avoided it but only just. It was not over, they turned around hearing dreadful screaming. Skylla had woken up. They drew their swords screaming with terror. Half of them suddenly disappeared, they vanished. A terrible crunching sound came from the cave as she ate them alive.

Michael Digby (14)
Bradfield College, Reading

A Day In The Life Of The Loch Ness Monster

This morning I woke up in my warm, cosy underwater cave in the middle of Loch Ness. I went to the opening of my cave and looked both ways. I looked up, made sure there were no boats with cameras coming to spy on me and went out. I hate that, I hate the fact that I have to hide from everyone and everything. Why am I so interesting? What have I done to make everyone want to see me? Don't they understand I just want to be left alone?

Anyway, I went out of my cave and just swam around for a bit. It's annoying that I can't find anything new to do in the whole Loch, yet I never get bored. I decided to take a risky trip to the surface. I was told by my father that it was more trouble that it was worth, but I still did it.

I like the surface, it's interesting looking at things out of water. I looked and then I saw a boy who was staring straight at me. I don't know why but I just stayed there and stared back. He looked scared and then his parents came so I left. I didn't do anything else that day.

Something told me that I just shouldn't.

James Peet (14)
Bradfield College, Reading

Section Of Powerless

Sarah's father walked over to Jake ready to hurt him as much as possible. How could such a man speak such lies, or worse, think them up? Jack moved, trying to be as far away from him as possible, knowing he had lost. What Sarah's father did not realise was that Jake was becoming very near to Sarah, so just as her father came close enough to harm him, Jake did something terrible.

He grabbed Sarah and placed a small dagger by her neck ready to slice it ... Everything seemed to be going so fast, one minute everything was going Sarah's father's way, now the tables had turned to Jake's fortune.

'Remember our deal, old man,' Jake sneered.

Oliver had become so scared at that moment, realising that his beloved Sarah could die very soon. He drew his sword willing to defend Sarah to his death. His undying love seemed the only thing that could protect Sarah now, for her father was in no position to do so. It looked as though Jake did not have a heart at all. For the other two men *loved* Sarah, while Jake, it seemed, only wanted her flesh. This cursed man was just that - cursed.

'You will release Sarah now or I will slay you on the spot!' He spoke with a sudden power that not even Sarah had heard.

'Sir, what are you doing?' Sarah's father asked, entirely confused. What did this nobleman think of Sarah? Her father did not think it possible that Oliver could feel something for her, yet this is what it certainly looked like. 'Remember our deal or death shall come to your daughter instead.'

Everything had gone terribly wrong. Suddenly in a flash the tables had turned and instead of saving Sarah, she was at the knife's edge.

'What bargain was this?' Oliver asked Sarah's father, begging not to hear the answer that her father would utter.

'He could have her for his own ... if he told us where to find her, I did not want this but it was the only way to find her, please forgive me Sarah,' he spoke almost in tears, realising his mistake.

Sarah had tears running down her face; she was utterly petrified, feeling the metal at her throat, not wanting to move an inch as that move could be fatal; she first looked at Oliver, knowing now that she had truly lost him, then to her father who loved her so much. Jake began to smell her hair and licked her face with his disgusting tongue, she strained not to retch as the evil man did this. Sarah slowly turned around to face Jake with pure hatred.

'I will never be yours ... the only thing you can do is kill me for that is all that I will allow you to have of me ... my death,' she spat the words out at him.

Jake looked back almost amused, did he think this all to be a joke? Then something he did not expect, a sudden pain exploded in his groin as Sarah kneed him hard. He fell down dropping the knife as he fell.

Sarah ran away from his side, straight into the arms of her love.

Alicia Lindsay (18)
Bradfield College, Reading

Myths And Legends

It all started on a Monday morning. Mr Berks had asked me for my English story. 'Right, boys. Now where are your English papers?' Everyone had handed something out except Sheldon who was known for not handing in work. 'Sheldon ... where's your work?' asked Mr Berks.

'Sir, there's a really funny story behind this.'

The teacher sat down and sighed waiting for the excuse.

'The thing is that ... umm ... I got robbed over the weekend.'

'Really?' the teacher said, not believing any of this false story.

'Yeah ... you see the shop was open and I was thinking of telling my story to the world, so I walked along the road. Then someone came up to me and put a water gun to my head and as I had a new haircut, my hair was not getting wet. So I said, 'Hey, I got a great essay if you want.' The man refused, sprayed me once with water and drove away.'

The teacher, by now, had opened a pack of prawn cocktail crisps and was munching at them while the children played their little games and some listened to the little story. 'Carry on, this is gripping ... really.'

Stefan F Heffron (14)
Bradfield College, Reading

Lady Of Shalott
(An extract)

Once upon a time there was a bustling town called Camelot. Nobody knew where it was actually located as it wasn't marked on any maps but Camelot was the prettiest of little towns. There were small cottages of which kind-hearted citizens of Camelot lived peacefully. The sky was always sapphire-blue, the sun always ripe. Everything about Camelot was cheerful. The young market girls dressed in red robes carrying their goods in a basket, the fair damsels whose husbands attended King Arthur and the strong reapers who harvested the crops.

Camelot was truly an undiscovered gem. But the government of Camelot was hiding a deep, dark secret. It was a secret so dark that it was hidden in the darkest tower of the darkest castle in the darkest area of the stream. The willows wept for the prisoner in the grey gloom of the castle on the isolated island of Shalott. This dark patch contrasted so heavily with the kaleidoscope of Camelot, yet nobody seemed to notice it. The island of Shalott lay in the middle of Camelot canal and was regularly passed by silken-sailed shallops or heavy barges, yet again the sailors never noticed the castle. The prisoner saw them all. Actually the prisoner saw their reflections and trapped them in a magical web.

The prisoner sat in the tower all day long, longing to be part of the outside world. Her only connection was a small rusted mirror which showed her images of Camelot. She was forbidden from leaving the castle and looking directly out of the window. This was her punishment for discovering that Queen Guinevere (the king's wife) and Sir Lancelot (the king's knight) were secretly having an affair behind King Arthur's back. She didn't mean to intrude but she just happened to overhear. So now, here she was weaving a blanket with colours and images that passed by the mirror - a blanket that would keep her warm at night.

Sayo Addous (13)
Cardinal Wiseman RC High School, Greenford

The Lady Of Shalott
(An extract)

The pale, sweet, sunlit sky shone brightly on the busy village of Camelot; the calm wind blowing the endlessly long dresses of the fair damsels and the manes of the knights' horses as they trotted carefree down the winding paths. Like a field of snow, the pure coloured lilies blew gently, sending their fragrant perfume through the warm breeze.

As the Lady of Shalott peered desperately and longingly into the enchanted mirror which revealed the affairs of the world outside, she recalled her misfortunate childhood.

The Lady of Shalott had been the result of an endless love affair between a young maiden and an extremely powerful warlock, thus granting their beautiful baby girl mystic powers. Since the child had been born out of wedlock, she was rejected by the townspeople and even more so as she was extremely spoiled and mischievous, abusing her inherited powers. She soon learnt how to place enchantments and spells on many of the other children in the village, which became a very destructive and worrying issue. Unfortunately, one bright summer's day, the young girl placed an enchantment on a witch's son. The witch was furious and as the terrified girl glared blankly into her cold, sharp, hypnotic eyes, her father's powers were slowly withdrawn from her. She was then locked away in a tower and a curse placed upon her. She would live there for eternity and only die when she broke the curse. Her death would be blood-curdling, tormenting and harrowing.

As she desperately tried not to imagine the hideous fate that would somehow, someway eventually be bestowed upon her, her pale, soft hands moved delicately, weaving whatever beauty she saw in the miraculously clean mirror beside her; the many fields of barley and rye with the reapers working tediously throughout the day. An old and weary-looking abbot in his draping robes ambled through the dusty paths passing the weeping willows and quivering aspens. A young shepherd with dark curly hair and a long-haired page in crimson showed in her enchanted mirror. The Lady of Shalott heaved a heavy sigh, 'I am half sick of shadows,' she whispered to herself as a tear rolled gently down her pale cheek.

Erika Scarth (13)
Cardinal Wiseman RC High School, Greenford

Overgrown
(An extract)

235 7th Ave, Inglewood - undoubtedly it stuck in my mind.

The warm red brick garden wall with its stocky mailbox perched on the end, like a patrol tower, stating in golden letters: 235. A small yellow plastic badge glued neatly next to the number boasted *Safety House,* the cartoon home beneath smiled in a gaudy yet welcoming manner, alerting passers-by of the fact that this place was part of the neighbourhood watch. Lush, crisp, tropical green grass grew avidly beneath the wall, both behind and in front, two tidily mown lawns, assisted by small, shiny black sprinklers, popping up when necessary, sudden and quick like a flea jumping. *Pop! Tick, tick, tick.* Whirring as they spun helicopters rotor blades regimentally delivering fresh, cool aid, keeping the grass smooth and chilled under foot.

Healthy shrubbery veiled the Tuscan terracotta bungalow, with its decreasingly visible veranda sitting unobtrusively beneath trees shading it from the harsh Australian sun. Trees smelling sweetly of the flowers they bore, trees dainty to the eye but strong to the touch, trees that supported many the young explorer. An old, faded red Ford Escort sat impatiently in the drive, not embarrassed of the many dints and scratches it bore, but boastful of its vital duties to the family who had never given up on it.

Behind the translucent mesh of the fly-screen door to the house, an icy fresh hardwood floor was the shock that initialised the body's journey from outdoor to in. Bare feet tingled beneath its sudden chill, as though stepping off lava onto ice. Next, eyes adjusted from the glare of the external radiance, and slowly adapted to the soft, unchallenging light inside the house. The ordinary hum of cicadas' regularly ticking faded and was readily replaced by the similar sounding chattering of several human voices.

A grand wooden sideboard, of the same strong dark wood of the floors, sat elegantly in the hall, showing off a great array of cheerful family photos, all tidily framed, some revealing small cracks, from being knocked over as children ran by, excited and careless. The first door led to a room filled with exotic mementos. Brightly coloured batik bedspreads from India; delicately carved wooden figures of animals from Indonesia; a jolly Thai Buddha made completely of stone; an assortment of intriguing, glimmering seashells; Malay temple-incense regularly burning, a mystical place, reminiscent of faraway lands.

Lydia Shellien-Walker (15)
Cardinal Wiseman RC High School, Greenford

Broken Bones
(An extract - the woeful tale of the unfortunate accidents of two siblings)

He totters along with the strange lopsided gait of a baby who has only recently learnt how to walk. His grubby face is smeared with a smile, giggles and high shrieks of happiness flowing from his mouth. His chubby cheeks are flushed, his dark eyes bright. He stumbles unsteadily towards my open arms.

The cold wind whips my face and tangles my hair. I fly past trees blown furiously by the wind, past the lake with great ripples disturbing the surface. A storm of ducks flies fluttering and flapping into the air as I pass, squawking their indignation to the skies. The tarmac is the stormy grey of the clouds above me, and it passes smoothly and swiftly beneath my skates. As the first drops of rain begin to patter around me, I throw my arms up and laugh wildly.

A step away from me he slips on the treacherously polished tile floor. He lands with a muffled thump, legs splayed in an awkward S-shape. For a moment there is silence, then he begins to cry. It starts as a quiet, low moan, gradually rising in pitch and volume to become a high-pitched wail, interrupted by a hiccup as he gasps for a breath.

'Mum!' I call as he continues to cry, panic rising in my voice.

She swoops in like an angel, hair disarrayed, flour smudged on her cheek, and sweeps him into her arms. Immediately the siren-wail stops, but his flushed cheeks drain of colour, his face turning the yellow-white of an old handkerchief. I feel his forehead: although icy cold, it is sticky and clammy. He moans and winces when Mum touches his left leg. 'Quickly, get your shoes on,' my mum tells me. 'We're going to the hospital.'

As I throw my arms up I trip over backwards and my feet, with their eight unruly wheels, go slip sliding from beneath me. As I topple, I flick my right arm out behind me, hoping to catch myself. I land on it strangely, and feel it crumple. Lightning bolts of agony rage from my wrist. I hold my arm up in front of me; it looks limp and unnatural. The movement causes twinges of pain to flicker momentarily. A scream rips unbidden from my throat. Moments later my dad is picking me up off the ground, gently reassuring, probing for details. I am cold, yet sweating, shivering madly. I can only whisper, 'My arm hurts.' He looked at it, a frown creasing his face. He picks me up in his warm arms, hugging me close to his chest.

'We're going to the hospital,' he says firmly.

Zoë Plant (15)
Cardinal Wiseman RC High School, Greenford

A Day In The Life Of My Guinea Pigs

It was a beautiful morning in the sun-drenched garden behind Nigel McKenzie's house. As the sun rose Dennis the guinea pig emerged from his bed in the hay. He got up on his small fat legs, waddled over to have a drink and waddled back again.

'What a peaceful life,' he said, as he settled down with his friend Bubbles on the warm, soft hay.

Around 11 o'clock Nigel McKenzie came into the garden, breathed in contentedly and said, 'What a lovely day for guinea pigs to be outside.' He picked them up and carried them to the run. Nigel was right, it *was* the perfect day to be outside. Dennis and Bubbles spent long hours grazing on the lush green grass as the sun's warmth spread all around them. Anyone would give up everything just to enjoy this warm and friendly atmosphere.

However, it did not last for long; a ginger cat got inside the run and gobbled up poor Dennis. Bubbles could not believe it, the atmosphere was terrible. A charming day in the garden changed to a deep, dark night in the graveyard at the sad loss of a friend. And as Bubbles sat there in the heartless pit of doom she said, 'It's not such a peaceful life after all …'

Mark Conway (14)
Kennet School, Thatcham

The Shouting Secret

'Cancer.' The word echoed around Emma's brain, a continuous scream in the darkness. As she sat in the consultation room, alone with her thoughts, Emma's body was rigid and still. Her face was pale, her mouth slightly open and a little bead of sweat slowly trickled down the side of her face. She clasped her hands together tightly, hoping and praying that she had heard wrong.

The room was cold and empty. A small shaft of light shone through the window and illuminated Emma's weary face. She glanced around the darkened room and sighed deeply. The smell was suffocating. The stale aroma of antiseptic seeped into Emma's lungs and she coughed quietly. Silence surrounded her, only to be broken by the sound of footsteps echoing along the adjoining corridor.

The afternoon set in and it was soon time for the school run. Emma stood outside the school gates, whilst a soft breeze gently lifted the hair off her forehead. The bell rang, and the playground was suddenly filled with the sound of chattering and laughter. As her two children bounded towards her, Emma struggled to hide her tears.

By nine o'clock Emma's secret had become almost like the cancer itself, controlling her every breath, thought and movement. She sat on the edge of the sofa, quietly rehearsing the lines in her head. The front door opened and her husband entered, completely oblivious to the day's events. Emma stood up and slowly approached him.

'I've got something to tell you,' she said …

Stephanie Marshall (15)
Kennet School, Thatcham

A Day In The Life Of A Field Medic In World War II

The neat row of cannons now stood silently. During the night there was a savage barrage on the landscape. The dust had ceased rolling over us but the fragments still lay smouldering all around. It was like Hell. And here was I, in a grey dawn, sewing bodies back together. I had worked through the night, person after person, body after body, corpse after corpse ... and my body was trembling with exhaustion.

The groan of ambulances with engines starved of petrol and care became quieter and quieter during the afternoon, but never quite stopped. Neat rows of battle-worn troops had been traipsing after their night shift. The sand-stained jackets clung to their deprived torsos while their rusted weapons had dangled from their necks.

I had done my shift and I had seen all the fractures and lacerations and haemorrhages; blood, guts and death. Scalpels were being cleaned by the dozen. A surgeon's nightmare ... my nightmare was the end of the surgical thread. A 'temporary thread' was just that - temporary. The bowel resection collapsed and a fifteen-year-old died of internal bleeding.

My uniform was still speckled with the blood of my fallen comrades and my skin seemed to be radiating the smell of death. My camo jacket was preferable to the 'clean' white overalls of the OR. Although worn with age, it was the closest thing to a home I had. The fighting had an effect on everyone; the eerie silence that shrouded the camp was refreshing: calm had swept over everyone.

Shaun Martin (15)
Kennet School, Thatcham

The Rampage Of The Bloodbean

Faith felt the warm breath of her friend Hope behind her as they tore away from the grip of the Bloodbean. Suddenly, it leapt upon Hope's back and feasted on her warm skin. It moved to the window of the old church, blood dripping from its sharp, protruding jaw.

Faith watched. The beast was small, about the size of a teddy bear. It was scaly and slimy with warts on its knees and elbows. Its eyes were a deep blood-red.

Last week an old farmer, Jack, and his dog Lassie were mangled and left hanging from the tallest oak tree. We found them. Now the town is full of fear. Everyone locks their doors.

Just then midnight struck and the Bloodbean changed into the form of Paolo, a small boy from the village. Faith screamed, he cried. She ran to help him.

'What's wrong? I don't understand!'

'I am cursed Faith. It's the Italian bullfighters' curse. My father fought bulls and caught the curse from a bull, Toro, murderer of thousands. Now I've got it. When the sun goes down I am Bloodbean, when midnight strikes I'm a boy. When Toro killed a man he would get powerful but when the man kills the beast they catch the curse.'

'Does your mother know?'

'Yes.'

'Come on!'

Faith took Paolo by the shoulders and led him home. His mother told Faith that she had chained him to a chair, but the chains were broken ...

Elouise Field (12)
Kennet School, Thatcham

Bills And Moon

Gertrude sighed as she arrived at the doctor's surgery and stepped up to the door.

Well, it's either this or going to the pharmacy and have everyone staring at you, Gertrude thought as she stepped through the door into the stark washed reception area. She approached the receptionist, who was too busy to notice her.

'Excuse me …' Gertrude muttered.

'What?' the receptionist barked.

'I'm here to see Dr …' Gertrude said.

'Oh, go and sit down. Your name will be called when he is ready,' the receptionist interrupted.

Gertrude strolled over to the bleached plastic chairs in the middle of the room. As she sat waiting, she drummed her fingers against the chair next to her.

'Miss G Alexander,' a tall handsome man called from the front of the room. Gertrude jumped when she heard her name called. She looked up and saw the most handsome man in the universe …

'Miss G Alexander,' he said again.

Gertrude stopped staring and walked slowly over to him taking in every detail. He wore a white doctor's coat. He had deep blue eyes which made her heart flutter and golden brown hair - very unusual for someone with blue eyes - which curled deliciously over his collar.

'Would you please come this way?' he said, pointing to a door.

Gertrude glided through the door and slumped into the seat. *How am I going to tell him about my foot?* Gertrude thought.

Trudi Hanson (13)
Kennet School, Thatcham

Sparrowhawk

A girl streaked through the gnarled trees of the forest, her long river-like hair tangling in the branches as she sped past, clutching a loaf to her chest. Two mounted soldiers ran after her, shouting threats and curses.

Soon the tiring child found a thorny bush and silently slid in-between its enclosing branches. The soldiers stopped, looking around, their horses snorting. Hidden, the girl's breath came in ragged bursts and she feared the men would hear her and take her to where rats and fleas nibbled at her toes, and spiders spun their intricate webs in her hair. At the thought the girl shuddered and the leaves keeping her safe twitched slightly. The soldiers immediately detected the movement and began thrusting their daggers into the mass of twigs. A soft growl was emitted from the middle of the bush.

A moment later, the large brown wolf came leaping out of the bracken and headed towards the men, snarling horribly. The horses whinnied in alarm, wheeled around and galloped away. The soldiers followed, clutching their scratched behinds.

The girl climbed out laughing, as the wolf turned and licked her face. Giggling, she pushed him down and stroked his silken coat, which was flecked with gold and chestnut streaks. The wolf, Sparrowhawk, barked a command and ran into the woods, his white tail showing like a beacon. The young girl jumped up and followed after him, disappearing like mist into the trees.

Samantha Friday (14)
Kennet School, Thatcham

A Day In The Life Of A Ghost

I'm so alone, and all on my own. There's no one to talk to when you're like me. My home's under the ground. They put me here on one special day. My wife comes to visit me, but she cannot see me, nor hear me.

Me and my wife were extremely close. Our love was vast, is vast. It still lives. My wife is pregnant. She carries my girl. I promised her I'd be there when she gives birth and we were going to bring her up. We would have silly arguments like who was going to feed her her first bottle, but she won't even be able to see me. She will never ever meet me. That makes me feel so incredibly guilty.

I sit in my home, just watching, simply watching at what my wife does. But she cannot see me. I watch her do everything. But the worst is when she cries and holds her bump. It makes me scream with sadness and anger that I am not there for her. 10 minutes, just 10 minutes to talk to her, and have her see me. My love is sat in front of me and I can't talk to her.

Our love is immense. It's so great. When I said 'I love you' she tingled and shook. I'm so infuriated with anger at the fact I'll never see her again. I'll never meet my baby. She will never meet me. Why didn't I look? It's so hard being dead.

Kimberley Buckland (14)
Langleywood School, Slough

Fabulous

'We're off!' said Linsey airily as she and her best friend Jenifer Lohan walked out the door.

Linsey Lopez had just turned fifteen and was being treated to a trip to Atlanta City to see Usher and Atl in concert. Linsey was a very shy girl and didn't do much to change that image. However, for once, Jenifer had talked her into wearing something different.

As Linsey and Jenifer walked around town wondering what they should do first, they saw Tina Knowles, Destiny's Child's designer.

Tina Knowles was mesmerised - she had turned around to see two pretty girls, one shy and one bold, you could tell by their outfits. They were perfect, she had needed two more girls for the modelling before the show (Usher's concert) and there they were.

Jenifer couldn't wait to change her hair and make-up for the show. Linsey, however, did not want to be in the show, she was too shy. However, she'd already promised and the limo was meeting them at 6.30, she had to be home by 8.30 but she didn't know why ...

Later ...

The limo arrived exactly on time; right after Jenifer had put her make-up on both herself and Linsey. As they bustled through the changing room trying to find Tina K, who would tell them what to do, they were steered towards the changing rooms. After changing into their first outfit Linsey rushed out towards hair and make-up, that's when she bumped into ...

Tenisha Trotman (14)
Langleywood School, Slough

A Day In The Life Of A Soldier

It all started as me and Kim sat in the history room listening to the teacher ranting on about how hard people had it in the war. All I could think of was my plans for that night.

All my plans were taken over by homework. Why did we care how people lived back then? Time had moved on, it was 2005. Be honest, what would you rather think of, now or then? All my plans were conceived due to homework. Logging onto a World War I site I felt myself change all of sudden. It was 1915 and I was a soldier called Bob with trench foot. I should have taken notice in history, at least then I could avoid being shot.

I felt a pain singe through my arm, without knowledge I fainted.

I awoke in hospital, or what was left of it. Soldiers were stood around me telling me what life had been like for them. I received a letter from home - the soldier I had become was a husband and father. His wife sent pictures, you couldn't read a lot of it as it'd been blacked out. What you could left tears in your eyes.

When I returned to my old self texting, I found myself writing a whole new viewpoint for my essay and understanding it. From that day on I never forgot what history has done for us and how it helped us get here today.

Sabrina Spicer (14)
Langleywood School, Slough

Lies

Maria and Tom were running around the roofs. Their demons flew above their heads. Heritha, Maria's demon, swooped down.

'The master is looking for you,' she exclaimed.

'Stuff him. I am having fun,' replied Maria.

'Maybe we had better be getting back,' said Tom sadly. 'I might be needed in the kitchen.'

'Oh fine,' said Maria, realising defeat. So the two children and their demons left.

When finally their feet touched the ground, the master came around the corner. 'Where have you been? I have been looking everywhere,' he asked.

Maria followed him. Heritha had her tail between her legs.

When they entered the master's library he said, 'Maria, who are your parents?'

'They died on that expedition ship,' Maria answered.

'No, we have been lying to you for your whole life. Your mother and father are alive. Your mother is widow Mortimer. Now the reason she is a widow is your father. He is a wonderful man but he killed her husband to protect you. His name is Lord Valdaram,' he said.

'No, Valdaram is my uncle not father!' Maria replied.

'That is not so, so you could be near him. Now Maria listen carefully to me, your mother is planning to do something terrible. You are the only one who can stop her,' he explained.

Maria sat down and wept bitterly. *Why does the whole world's existence always rely on me?* she thought. For if Maria decided not to help, the world would be destroyed.

Lynsey Johnston (14)
Langleywood School, Slough

Hercules' Revenge

The wind blew fiercely, the howl sounded like screams. I struggled through the mountain, every step felt like a mile long. I approached a cave in the mountains, Mount Doom. Mount Doom was the passage to the Underworld and to Heaven. I have come here to seek for help. I shout out, 'Ra, oh Ra, help me for Hades has taken my soul. I beg you.'

A deep rumble from the sky, it flashed like a camera, yet rumbled like herd of elephants. A voice shouted out form the sky, 'You will have your soul back if only you defeat the army of the Underworld.' I agreed.

'Hades come up here and attack me.' The ground shook beneath my feet like a tremendous earthquake. A crack appeared, out of the crack fire flamed out, furiously. The army marched out of the crack one by one. The army was huge. I needed help. I bellowed out my battle cry, the nearest heroes appeared, the cyclops with the super strong laser eye, and the swift dragon. Along with the strong Minotaur and the ugly death-defying Medusa, us five against the army of the Underworld.

The dragon swooped up and annihilated most of them, along with the Minotaur who crushed them, the cyclops who cut them in half and Medusa turned the rest to stone. Only a few enemies left, it was my go, as the others were tired. I jumped in and slashed off arms, heads and everything else. We were victorious. I returned to Mount Doom and had my soul returned. I felt alive.

Jamie Whittington (13)
Langleywood School, Slough

Everlasting Pain

What is the meaning of life? Are we destined to struggle in this world, full of hatred, only to breathe one's last? Why do we strive to achieve so much, when all will be lost? Here is a story of a girl, best known as Maria, how her questions of life ... became the downfall of her.

Everything came in focus when Maria's parents died. Snatched coldly from her life ... she began to question everything she believed so dearly. Why would God allow such a thing? Why? If there was a guardian angel watching over ... why would it destroy her so?

The light that had once sparked such ambition into Maria's eyes, had vanished. She was now a walking zombie, fearful of what else life may destroy. Maria's world was shattered into a thousand pieces, never to be repaired. Confusion surrounded her. Pain surrounded her. She became suffocated on life itself. The burden to smile became too much for her, simply too much. No longer could she keep the pain locked inside her heart, she had to release it, somehow.

And so tragically, Maria killed herself on December 25th, Christmas Day.

What a shame it is, the loss of a beautiful girl. She was destined to go great things, but now she'll never sing. This story is true, not a myth.

Amunpreet Bains (14)
Langleywood School, Slough

Knock, Knock You Stink

'Knock, knock!' shouted Chris.
'Who's there?' whispered Ross.
'Luke!'
'Luke who?'
'Luke through the keyhole and see,' Chris burst out laughing, but Ross just stood there.
'That ... was not ... funny,' said Ross.
Chris then turned around to see Colin Zas.
'You are really unfunny Christopher. Just watch me make those girls over there laugh their socks off,' said Colin. He walked up to the girls, the weirdest way ever. 'Hey girls.'
'Hi Colin,' said all the girls at once.
'Knock, knock!'
'Who's there?'
'Luke.'
'Luke who?'
'Luke through the keyhole and see.'
After about 10 seconds they laughed.
'You see Chris, that is how you tell a joke,' said Colin.
'Ross, I'm gonna kick Colin Zas.'
'Hey, that's not funny!' cried Colin, running into the toilets.

The next day Chris was on his way to school. He had to carry all his books. He tripped over and all his stuff went in a puddle.
'I've got a good joke,' said a man who just walked up.
'What do you call a homeless snail? A slug!'
'Ha, that's really good, my name's Chris.'
'My name's Daniel Carmichael and this is my partner in comedy, Mark.'
'Hello,' said Mark, appearing from behind a lamp post.
Chris told everyone the jokes he'd heard. Every day Chris met up with Daniel and got the jokes, then told everyone, they were a hit, then one day Colin noticed Chris being told the jokes. Then for a while Chris did all of Colin's homework, in exchange for not telling. Then Colin got sent away.

Daniel Keates (13)
Langleywood School, Slough

Friend Finally Found

Creepy, absolutely creepy. I entered the dark destination deep beneath the narrow never-ending stairs. I was outside yet another huge door, with lots of cobwebs hanging from it. Here, I knew I would find out the truth.

I was trembling on the spot, I started to sweat. Before I knew it I was getting hot - extremely hot, but I had to do it, I had to open the door, this lighthouse seemed to make me feel claustrophobic.

I clenched my fist, took hold of the door handle then twisted ... I couldn't believe my eyes, I just couldn't. There, right in front of me, was my long-lost dead friend - the mystery which still remains unsolved.

I was frightened, terrified ... waiting to get out ... instantly. I ran as fast as I could, towards the door, wanting to get away. Suddenly the wind blew through the creaky window ... the door slammed - there was no way out!

I stood in the corner of the dim, dusty room, I started to cry, tears were dripping one by one from my unaware face. I cried and cried. Before I knew it there was a puddle on the floor. My legs were becoming tired, I crouched down, curled up in a ball, sat in the puddle, drowning my sorrows.

The room was getting smaller and smaller, I had no space to breathe, let alone think. I was becoming tired. I lay down on the cold, creepy floor - waiting to be found ...

Sunil Ram (14)
Langleywood School, Slough

The Chase

The last twenty-four hours were hell. He had run through Gibraltar for the past three hours before they'd given up.

It had all started in Paris where Will was driving around in his Hummer. His companions were in the other fast SUVs. They knew they were being followed. They managed to get to the outskirts of Paris when they gave chase.

For eight hundred miles, they drove through the French countryside until they reached the Spanish border. Will, Bill, Phil and Dill did not have their passports. Phil saw a parked up car transporter and radioed the others. They moved their cars in line with the ramp and revved their engines. Will went first. Over the border he went cruising in the air. The car hit the road with a thud. The others followed.

Their followers continued until they saw the Spanish border with Will Bill, Phil and Dill on the other side. They were lucky. The border made them give up.

Will and his companions had some new chasers. The Spanish police. With the Spanish now on them the drive became more fun. The team decided to split up and head for Gibraltar.

Will took the shortest route and landed in Gibraltar first. The police were still on him. What he didn't realise was that a stinger had been placed up ahead. He swerved, hitting a wall. He jumped out and ran. He ran until the police gave up. His friends finally caught up and saved him.

Mark Taylor (14)
Langleywood School, Slough

The Loch Ness Monster

Splish, splosh, splish, splosh.

I slowly started to hear a soft, strange sound on the surface of the ocean. I got out of my car to get a better look, only to find the needle-sharp raindrops stung my eyes so much they were glued shut.

All of a sudden the waves rippled, one after another, *ripple, ripple, ripple*. What was it? Where was it? Who was it? I couldn't see it. Then a pause ... *Awww!* There it was. The myth everyone was talking about. The Loch Ness monster.

It looked like a whale, but with the neck of a giraffe. It was a greeny-yellowish colour with bright red splodges around its midriff. *Awww!* There it was again. The almighty roar. It was like a young child screaming when she isn't allowed a toy she has seen in the shop.

1, 2, 3, then it was gone. I was astounded! I was one of the lucky people to grace upon the one and only Loch Ness monster.

Michael Hooton (14)
Matthew Arnold School, Oxford

Saint George And The Dragon

I will never forget the ruby-red eyes the mighty beast had or the day that I came upon the devilish dragon of doom.

It was a bleak winter's morning and I had just ridden into the so-called Land of Fire. The stench of burnt and rotting corpses had entered my nostrils like a furious fever. I sensed by its unease that it had reached the silver stallion's nose too. Then, suddenly, from behind a roasted tree the creature of many people's nightmares appeared! It stared at me as if trying to distract or hypnotise me, then unexpectedly it reared up on its back legs and charged.

The battle between man and myth had begun. Before I knew it my horse was swept from beneath me and impaled upon my own sword, I was left stranded on the arid dirt with only an axe and rope. Immediately I began to dodge what would have been fatal blows from the dragon's tail that had a barb at the end as sharp as a thousand skewers. In a moment of inspiration I fixed the rope and axe together. I started to spin the contraption around my head. When this rotated it buried deep into the beast's face, leaving two blood-drenched trenches behind. The overgrown lizard started to make a deafening sound like a squealing pig as it hit the floor like a sack of bricks.

It was dead!

Jamie Cummings (14)
Matthew Arnold School, Oxford

Daedalus And Icarus

Something that's as bad as Apocalypse has happened to me today. This is an outstanding, upsetting event in any man's life. This is the worst thing that could happen to me and I am afraid, I am appalled, I am initiated into Hell.

We'd been locked in the king's tallest tower for far too long so I, being the great Daedalus the inventor, thought of the great plan, greater than God.

The next morning I started stripping the feathers from the pillows like a monkey who had not eaten for years, peeling a banana. Once I had got all the feathers, I got the honey from the hidden area under the floorboards.

Half an hour later my son Icarus had beautiful birds' wings. I then warned him about getting too close to the sun but idle Icarus didn't listen, he never did, that stupid, ignorant boy.

He then flew out the window like an archangel advancing to Heaven. He then flew higher and higher and higher. I screeched at him to not go any higher but would he listen? No! Then it happened. The idle, ignorant Icarus got too high and too close to the sun. He fell. He fell like a parachutist with no parachute. I was afraid.

Then he hit the ground with a bone-crunching and bloody squelch. I had to look down at his bloody, bleeding, broken body.

I will be proud of my idle, ignorant Icarus for eternity.

Michael Hodges (14)
Matthew Arnold School, Oxford

Perseus And Medusa

Was it me? Did I do this? I can't believe I did it, yes! She's dead. When I heard that final screech I knew I'd got victory, as if I'd won the war.

She was most feared by people, no one wanted to look at her and face a painful death by being turned to stone.

It all started when I was bombarded by a random old man shouting and screaming, 'Help me! Help!' You could see that he was horrified. Then he said it, 'There's a monster in there with snakes for her hair!'

I got my sword and my shield and went straight in. She was there, standing with the snakes for her hair. With the mirror I had I shoved it in her face. With that, a horrifying screech. That was it, she was dead and I am still here.

Alex Gibson (14)
Matthew Arnold School, Oxford

The Truth About The Loch Ness Monster

The Loch Ness monster became popular because people kept saying that they'd seen it, but nobody has really seen or taken a picture of this incredible beast. I know this because it is a flying animal, it is actually quite small, in fact only about three metres square.

Nobody knows which sex it is but I have reason to believe it is both because it had a baby and it is no large monster. Sadly the offspring did not make it.

This creature is my favourite animal because it is so beautiful and harmless. Its white feathers glisten in blue, pink and green, much like an opal. It also has dark purple eyes which look like glass.

This monster has no name, has no home, no food. Is it me or am I going mad?

Bryony Rose (11)
Matthew Arnold School, Oxford

Hercules Meets Shrek

It all started at Shrek's swamp where Hercules had lost his way. As usual Donkey was singing while Shrek was trying to make him shut up. Suddenly there was a knock at the door. When Shrek opened it, there was a muscular man standing in front of him.

'Hi, I'm Hercules, my trailer broke down. Could I stay at your house for a couple of days?'

'Well,'

'Of course you can,' Fiona said, before Shrek said no.

Over the days, Shrek and Hercules did not get on well. Hercules thought that Shrek was disgusting and Shrek thought Hercules was too clean.

After a week they both snapped. It was going to be the biggest fight ever, but then a rock came flying through the window. It said: 'Bring me Donkey or you'll never see your precious Fiona again. From the King of Lardieland'.

Of course Shrek doesn't give in to threats easily, so he got all of the fairy-tale creatures that he knew and Hercules got all of his friends and they all went off to save Princess Fiona.

When they got to Lardieland there were hundreds of soldiers waiting for them, but it didn't take them very long to narrow it down to just the king, partly because half of the soldiers ran away. All Hercules had to do was look at the king and he was gone in a flash.

After that, Hercules and Shrek became friends and didn't fight ever again.

Spencer Ramsay (12)
Matthew Arnold School, Oxford

A Day In The Life Of A Soldier In The First World War

5.15am

I'm at the front line ready to fire, my finger on the trigger. All the men are under pressure, we've been like this for 15 minutes. It's all quiet, too quiet apart from the constant scream of wounded soldiers. I myself am a private. I feel homesick. Some of the soldiers are crying because they miss someone.

7.25am

We're sustaining heavy fire, probably from the big guns, it looks like the war's in action. I've been called up and a couple of other men, we've been told to take out the Jerry guns, the big guns, this mission is called Pistol Pete. It is named after the captain that is coming with us.

9.45am

We left the trenches an hour ago, we have travelled about 7 miles. There's isn't mud anymore, like where the trenches are, there is tall straw-like grass and we have to crouch down so no Jerries can see us. There is a wood in the distance. 'It will be good camouflage,' said the captain.

11.55am

We have set up base so we can rest and look out for Jerries I was on the outskirts of the base in the woods where I saw a big gun. I whispered to the other men; we went in and took the place over with all the Jerries surrendering. We had succeeded.

Greg Terry (12)
Matthew Arnold School, Oxford

An Alternative Chapter To 'Holes'
(In the style of Louis Sachar)

Zero returned and carried on digging. Ten minutes later he finished and went to have his shower. Instead of letting him shower, the counsellors took Zero to the warden.

'Excuse me!'

'Here is Zero, we found him at the showers.'

The warden moved towards Zero and viciously struck him with her nails. Zero fell to the floor.

When all the boys were eating, Zero came in. They all fell silent. Nothing happened. Zero began to eat. Still nothing happened.

The next morning when everyone was out digging, Caveman asked Zero if he was OK.

'Tonight is the night!' whispered Zero. 'Save your lunch and make sure you have water and when everyone's done digging, we'll go.'

Later when everyone had gone in ...

'Now's our chance.'

Step
    step
        step
           step.

Slowly but surely they walked across the lake, towards *God's Thumb*, dodging holes as they walked.

'Zero, what happened to your face?'

'The warden struck me with her nails.'

As they headed towards the mountain, Caveman saw a yellow spotted lizard that Zero did not see as it came closer
                      and
                          closer
                              until ...

Ouch!

Zero fell to the floor. Caveman did not want to leave him so he lifted him onto his shoulder and carried him.

Caveman walked all night and had to rest, he drank the last of the water and set off again. Soon after, they reached the top.

'Caveman, I felt a drop of rain!'

Emma Livett (13)
Matthew Arnold School, Oxford

An Alternative Chapter To 'Endgame'
(In the style of Chris Wooding)

'Hello and welcome to Channel 4 news. As the impending conflict draws nearer, many people are wondering how we can try to survive the nuclear blasts. Here with me is Doctor Steven Heavenage. Doctor, what can we expect to be able to do if NATO's plans fail?'

'Well Sarah, you will need to make suitable shelters in your house, by leaning doors and mattresses against a wall and stocking up on provisions.'

Mayner, Kayleigh, Wren and Jamie were all hanging out in the café at the Vil. All of them were silent. The media had finally realised that there was an impending war at hand here and were telling people how to protect themselves.

'I thought you said no one would dare have a war nowadays,' said Kayleigh.

Silence.

'Hello?' Kayleigh continued. 'Anyone listening to me?'

Silence.

She noticed Jamie and Wren were both sharing the headphones of Wren's personal radio. They looked terrified.

'What's wrong?' asked Kayleigh, afraid of the answer.

'Well,' said Wren, 'the army are calling for all young, able-bodied men to come and join the armed forces.'

'They can't make us!' shouted Jamie suddenly. 'No one can force me to go out and die ...'

'Jamie ...'

'No!' Suddenly, Jamie jumped up and stormed out of the café, leaving his stunned friends behind him, forever.

Thomas Connick (13)
Matthew Arnold School, Oxford

An Alternative Chapter To 'Holes'
(In the style of Louis Sachar)

The day Stanley escaped, Mr Sir died. Seemingly a normal day, the boys would dig a five-foot hole each then they would rest indoors. No one expected Mr Sir to be bitten by a yellow spotted lizard.

Stanley had been planning to escape for weeks. Every night he would add more to his tunnel. Every time he went to the toilet he would add more to his tunnel. Every time he was close to a shovel he would add more to his tunnel. Then Mr Sir saw him. 'What are you doing?' he asked.

Stanley shrugged one arm.

'Well look here, a tunnel,' Mr Sir exclaimed. 'You wouldn't be trying to escape, would you Caveman?'

'No Mr Sir,' Stanley replied.

'You wouldn't be trying to dig for gold would you Caveman?'

'No Mr Sir,' Stanley replied.

'For water?'

'No Mr Sir.'

Stanley's shovel was standing in the dirt. He lunged and tried to smack Mr Sir but Mr Sir caught it. Stanley swung his shovel in an arc but Mr Sir caught it again. Nobody saw the yellow spotted lizard on the shovel. Mr Sir died. Stanley started shaking, he hadn't wanted to kill Mr Sir, just wound him, but he had. Then a fear-borne idea came to Stanley.

Stanley's original plan was to lay his leisure clothes in the dirt to make the driver and guard come out, leaving him to steal the bus. Now he had a better idea.

Stanley lay Mr Sir on the road. He then dug a semi-circle ditch around Mr Sir and covered it with his ripped leisure clothes. Stanley waited.

Tick.

Tock.

Tick.

Tock.

Ti ... the bus arrived. As planned, it screeched to a halt.

'Jesus!' exclaimed the driver.

The guard leapt out of the bus and sprinted to Mr Sir. He yelped as he tripped over the ditch. *'Aaarrrgggghhhiieee!'* he screamed, 'I think I sprained it.'

The driver ran to the guard.

Stanley snuck into the bus. He slammed his foot on the accelerator. The bus driver, toting the guard's shotgun, shrieked and ran after the bus. He fired two bullets. Both missed. After that he tripped on a rock.

Stanley drove into the sunshine.

David Owen (12)
Matthew Arnold School, Oxford

A Day In The Life Of Kelly Holmes

I train hard every day and try to keep fit. As part of my sport I try to help kids keep fit too by telling them to eat healthy foods. I eat quite a lot, you might not think so but I eat mainly healthy foods.

Every day I train with my trainer and I train with other athletes too. We all try and help each other train hard to win the races or the long jump and other great sports like that.

Every day we put our muscles to the test so that we can win gold in the finals. We have to get up early to start training and don't stop until it's dark. We don't drink much alcohol so we can keep our bodies in good condition.

On the day of the race we get up early to start exercising and work-outs. Then we can start to run round the track to get to understand it and the shape of it. Then before the race we do our last exercises, have a drink, get into position and then we're off.

After the race we sit and get our breath back and have a drink and talk about how we think we did. Then we wait for our results to find out who's won gold, silver and bronze. Then we go up for our medals, go home, have a bath or shower and then go to bed ready for the next day.

Stephanie Mileson (12)
Matthew Arnold School, Oxford

Myths And Legends

I hid behind the corner of the old barn and I watched as the two slaves came out from what looked like an old dungeon. The dungeon gate slammed shut. *Thumb!* and the two slaves disappeared into the darkness of the night.

As soon as the coast was clear, I ran over. I was able to slip through the gap between the gate and the wall. I was as quiet as a rat but as quick as a knight on a horse. I found a lighted torch so I took it with me as I started to follow the tunnel as it went further and further underground. The further I walked, the more I felt like what I was doing was a bad thing, but still I walked on.

I noticed that there was something strange on the floor; I couldn't see what it was so I moved part of it, only to realise that it was an old, skinless skeleton. Now this really started to scare me, all different thoughts started rushing through my head but I could see a light at the end of the tunnel so I kept on.

The next room was huge! From the books I was guessing it was a library. It was as big as a castle and definitely the biggest I'd seen. I walked over and picked up an old book when suddenly, *thumb!* A book had been knocked on the floor. I slowly walked over and picked it up, when I started to hear some heavy breathing behind the bookcase. I found and picked up a shiny, stylish sword. My heartbeat started to rise. I rushed round the bookcase and you wouldn't believe what I saw. It was a dragon, a young one who was very shy and nervous. Who would ever know that this dragon and I would become the best of friends and would be friends for life?

Hayley Trendell (14)
Matthew Arnold School, Oxford

The Werewolf

It was starting to get dark and the moon was coming out, I only stepped off the path for a moment and then I heard it, *oh no!* It was getting closer, closer, it suddenly all went dark. All I could feel was a pain. It was so excruciating it was all I could think about! What was going on?

This beast was on me eating away and I couldn't do anything about it! I felt so useless, I was so sure I was going to die. A werewolf was attacking me and I didn't know why!

My eyes were opening and all I could see was this blinding white light. I had very bad pain all over my body. I must have blacked out or something. I had no idea what had happened!

When I sat up I got a creepy, cold shiver going through my back. I thought to myself, *what will I do, where will I go?* I was miles away from home.

There was a river nearby so I went down and washed in the river. I didn't know what I was going to tell my wife, I would be hung before the next full moon!

I started on my long journey home and from that day on I came to that very spot to take my place as a werewolf when the full moon came out!

Riziki Summers (14)
Matthew Arnold School, Oxford

Sword In The Stone

I watched them all and I watched them all fail. As they wandered off down to the alehouse, the noise they made was terrible. It was like a sky full of growling monsoon clouds. Each one of them was disappointed. The sword had failed them.

The whining winter wind was cold that day. I wrapped the woollen scarf tighter. The knights and warriors were slow and careful on the thick brown mud. Their gleaming, colourful armour was their pride. If one was to slip and fall, then that pride would be taken. The men's long hair was beautifully combed, they shone like rays of sunlight and floated like flags in battle. I thought they looked like elegant stallions, each one graceful but stubborn.

Eventually I was alone. I sniffed. The air was cold and the breeze was icy. I looked at the sword in the stone and wondered.

Like a fox after the hens, I crept towards the sword at the top of the hill. The wind swept me up the hill, a wave pushing a fishing boat to shore.

A string loosened around a sack of feelings, excitement set free, curiosity escaped and fright eased its way out.

At the top of the hill I stared at the sword. Could there be anything more beautiful? A gem the colour of a young hound's eyes glinted its clear blue. Surrounding it was an army of shining stars. Entwining the stones was the cold Celtic pattern made of the rare and mysterious platinum, but the blade itself was the core of everything.

A shout came up from the alehouse. Someone had spotted me. Should I run down or pull out the sword? Now there was a group of cries, in desperation I grasped the sword.

Then it shifted.

Sophie Cook (12)
Matthew Arnold School, Oxford

The Sinking Of Atlantis

My life has been washed away and I can't do anything about it. I'm sitting on a small rock, with a black fist of guilt welling up inside of me. I can't believe what I've just done. All around me is the wreckage of Atlantis and I can still hear people calling for help. But I dare not try to rescue them, for fear of being swallowed up by some monster of the deep.

My young sister, Isca and I were playing with a small figurine made out of thousands of tiny shells when the rumbling started. At first it was as quiet as a whisper but it got louder and louder with every passing second, until it was deafening. Isca looked at me with more terror than I had ever seen before. 'The wrath of Poseidon!' she screamed. 'Run!'

But there was nowhere to run. Atlantis was an island, cut off from the rest of the world.

Then I saw it. A rapidly moving blue-green wall of water, bringing with it an overpowering salty smell. I grabbed onto a sturdy timber post, which kept me anchored as the ice-cold water slammed into me.

Isca was not so lucky. She reached out a hand desperately as she was thrown past, but I did not grab it. I was too scared, and I had to watch my little sister being swept away by the waves.

That is how I got here, but what hope is there of getting back?

Freya Bower (11)
Matthew Arnold School, Oxford

The Lair Of Kamassooki

As Arthur reached the entrance of the cave where the dreaded Kamassooki's lair was, his heart was pounding like a parade of drummers. It was said that Kamassooki was a ferocious monster, the size of a house. Soon, Arthur would find out for himself.

He crept through the winding passages of the cave, his head peering round each corner. Slowly and slyly as if a thousand knights were waiting to attack, he heard a load roar echo throughout the cave. He knew he was close. Finally he turned his head round the last corner and there stood the famous Kamassooki.

It was at least 10 feet tall. It was round with skin like a beach of pebbles and eyes the size of tennis balls. Its tail was as long as 5 snakes joined together.

Thump, thump, thump. The cave vibrated and Arthur struggled to move. The monster picked him up with its gigantic arm. Arthur clenched his sword in his right hand and stabbed into the monster's forearm. It screamed so loudly Arthur's ear lost all hearing for a few minutes. Then Arthur swung at its neck and its head flew off. Blood gushed out of its body like a fountain. The fight was over and Arthur was victorious.

David McIver (12)
Matthew Arnold School, Oxford

King Midas' Mistake

Oh my gosh. I am as rich as the most richest king that has lived to this very day. I may have all the wonders of the world just at the touch of my hand. I can eat off golden plates. I may turn brick into gold and gravel into any amount of money. But now it is time for me to relish my daily supply of holy food. As I sit down on my old wooden chair it turns into gold.

All of a sudden I have a beautiful feeling to help out those less fortunate than I. As I hold my fork it turns to gold. I start to feel awkward. What if this happens to my food? As I hold my goblet it turns into a golden goblet. I hold the clear liquid within to my lips and as I do it too turns solid. So I can't drink. Let me see if I can eat. No. Oh no, whatever I touch turns into solid gold. Oh no.

I hear the front door opening. My wife and children are back. I must warn them not to touch me.

My daughter is coming, she is running wildly like some animal catching prey. She runs and gives me the blessing of a grateful hug. As she does she turns to gold. My beautiful, young, loving daughter.

Kiranjit Kamal (12)
Matthew Arnold School, Oxford

Theseus And The Minotaur

'I shall return,' I stated boldly and entered the labyrinth. As the darkness grabbed me, I felt a cold breeze, that chilled my already nervous soul. As I was creeping through the labyrinth my awareness sharpened. There are rotting corpses everywhere, those of the prisoners who died in honour against the Minotaur and all those who didn't dare. I still do not understand why I wanted to enter this hazardous maze. I must be insane. Wait, what's this? I think I've found the very heart ... Then, all of a sudden, the Minotaur, leapt out from behind a wall, scaring me to death.

I fell back, just in the amazement of the sheer sight of the beast. The air was foul, being so close to the centre of the labyrinth. Now I was back on my feet and then it began. We both charged and were locked in mortal combat. I only realised its skill as I began to fight. It nearly took my head off three times. This was going to be more of a challenge than I expected and I feared for my life.

After minutes of combat my leg was severed off and I fell, bleeding to the floor. As the Minotaur moved in for the kill, I lunged and pierced its heart with my sword. It fell like a cripple but was not dead. I felt its fear as I raised my sword and swiped. I had won. But as relief took over, I then lost consciousness.

Ben Hackett (12)
Matthew Arnold School, Oxford

The Return Of Odysseus

There she is. She's looking at me now. Straight through me. She doesn't recognise me; obviously. I have my cloak on which is ragged and torn. I must look different after 20 years of being at war. Also, Athene made me look old as a better disguise. I must get ready. The contest will be starting soon.

It is now my turn. I have my bow after sneaking into the palace to get it. Thank the gods it is an archery contest; I may not win her back otherwise. There are thousands of people, over half of Ithica, here to witness the finding of their new king. I hope that I will get her back.

As I step up to the platform, my heart begins to race like a cheetah and I feel it going so fast; it nearly stops. As I reach out for an arrow, I catch a glimpse of my beauty. I must win this contest!

I fasten my arrow into my bow and then let it go. As I do this, my cloak slips and slides off me. I am doomed to Hades. Everyone is staring at me. Do they know who I am? Penelope is also looking, staring, confused. She knows who I am. I can see it in her eyes.

'Odysseus, is it really you? Have you returned?'

'Yes my love. I have returned. I have been guided, loved by the gods and I am here now; in front of you.'

Shannen Bound (12)
Matthew Arnold School, Oxford

Colin's Diary

(Colin is a character from a book we have been reading in class called 'Two Weeks with the Queen'. Luke, Colin's brother, has just fainted and been admitted to hospital)

Thursday 25th December 2004

This has been the worst Christmas ever. Not only did Luke get all the best presents and all the attention (surprise, surprise!). He's gone and landed himself in hospital just because he ate too much, (as usual). Mum and Dad are fussing over Luke so much that I've got to stay with my nan tonight while they're at the hospital.

Even if I was ill, Mum and Dad would still fuss over Luke, they'd just say that *I'd* eaten too much. There hasn't been anything good about today apart from meeting the doctor, I could go and live with him because he's got a Jag and two sprinklers, whereas we've only got a rusty old motor and a leaking hosepipe. Maybe if I went and lived with him he'd buy me a new microscope with seven different 200m focuses like the one Mr Blair has got.

Today started alright, well - fine, the first two minutes were OK. But after Luke got the Mig fighter plane and I got the horrible shoes that give you blisters, everything went downhill. I didn't even enjoy Christmas dinner because Luke got most of the turkey nuggets, most of the potatoes, most of the parsnips, most of the pigs in blankets *and* most of the Chrissie pud. I got stuck with a plateful of vegetables and a bowlful of custard. No wonder I'm practically wasting away. I hope tomorrow is better.

Colin Mudford

PS Did I tell you what Josh got for his birthday? A PlayStation! A PlayStation, he is soooo lucky. I wish I was him.

Jessica Ballard (12)
Matthew Arnold School, Oxford

Theseus And The Minotaur

Oh the stench. The stench of rotting flesh! I could hardly breathe. It was as if I was in a room full of toxic gas, struggling for every breath.

As soon as I entered the dark, dismal maze, I cannot begin to describe what I could see. Oh, the horrific sight! Bodies everywhere, scattered like seeds. Bones everywhere I looked! But that was nothing compared to what I was faced with next.

The Minotaur, with metre-long horns like heavy steel poles and human flesh dangling out of his mouth. Blood ran down his neck like a polluted waterfall. I would rather have died than fought that hideous thing! But something stopped me, something from deep inside, I had to do it. If not for anyone else, for my father!

As I heroically launched myself at the Minotaur, I could see my whole life flash before my eyes.

I grappled with the Minotaur, a fearsome monster, then grabbed it by the horns and yanked them. I heard an ear-piercing scream, I looked down. I had pulled off one of the Minotaur's horns! I then knew what to do. I plunged the horn into the Minotaur's neck, there was another blood-curdling shriek!

Slowly the Minotaur collapsed and formed a huge twitching mass on the floor.

I was victorious!

Joe Jenkins (14)
Matthew Arnold School, Oxford

An Alternative Chapter To 'Holes'
(In the style of Louis Sachar)

Stanley stumbled slowly through the desert.
'Water,' he cried weakly.
He glanced up and saw something orange and hazy flicker across the edge of his vision.
'Water,' he croaked.
He could not tell what it was.
'Water,' he said again. Or would have if he wasn't face down in the dirt.
Somebody was leaning over him, asking him to wake up. But he did not want to wake up.
He did not want to find himself stuck in the middle of a desert.
He did not want to have to carry on searching for Zero.
And he did not want to go back to Camp Green Lake.
Plus he was having the most delicious dream about an ice cream sundae. The sundae felt cool and refreshing against his parched lips. The sun was bright, but not unpleasant like Camp Green Lake. How easy it would be just to forget about the earth and slip towards the light. Towards the light and forget everything. Towards the light.
Suddenly the refreshing ice cream sundae was replaced by foul-tasting water, trickling into his mouth from a dirty canister, which led up to an orange clothed body, to a face, wreathed in matted, frizzy hair, until Stanley was staring into the twinkling eyes of Zero.
Zero burst out laughing. Stanley wondered why Zero was laughing, but just seconds later found himself laughing too, at the sheer joy of having finally found Zero.

Robert Whitelock (13)
Matthew Arnold School, Oxford

An Alternative Chapter To 'Holes'
(In the style of Louis Sachar)

Stanley was escaping. He knew that it was dangerous but he could not stand it anymore. The work, the heat, the everything. It was too much.

X-ray heard Stanley get up. *Idiot, he'll be back,* thought X-ray.

He was right.

Again.

Silently, Stanley crept out of D Tent and made his way to the shower block. Stanley stopped, in the middle of the path was a yellow spotted lizard.

Stanley stood still, frozen to the spot. The lizard looked at him and walked off. Stanley breathed a sigh of relief and went to fill his canteen.

Stanley heard a rustling noise. He prayed it wasn't a yellow spotted lizard. Stanley turned around, there was nothing there. *No one would get up at this time of night,* thought Stanley.

Unluckily for him someone did get up.

Mr Sir got out of bed to see if he could shoot anymore yellow spotted lizards. He saw Stanley creeping towards the mess hall. He turned back to go to bed, he did not want to upset the warden.

Again.

Then he saw Stanley coming out of the mess hall with a bag of sunflower seeds.

His seeds.

Stanley heard the gunshot.

Hot fire seared up Stanley's leg. Stanley stumbled forward a few steps, then collapsed to the floor.

Stanley had done it.

He had failed.

Again.

Jack Leahy (13)
Matthew Arnold School, Oxford

An Alternative Chapter
(To 'Mates, Dates and Sleepover Secrets' in the style of Cathy Hopkins)

I walked over to Nesta and Lucy the following day at school. I hoped they were not going to be horrible and tell everyone what I'd told them. Oh I wish Hannah was here. If only she hadn't been dragged off to Africa then she could have given me support.

As normal Nesta was looking fabulous. Today she had her hair in bunches, she was wearing blue eyeshadow with bright red lipstick to match, the colour of her cheeks. She was flirting with a Year 11 when I came over.

Surprisingly they did not have that guilty look on their faces, which they had when they had done something bad, like dump a boy just because they fancied another one. So I carried on walking over to them and they were fine. The rest of the day was great, I had all the boys flirting with me. I couldn't believe it, boys flirting with me. TJ Watts. I couldn't wait to get home and tell Hannah:

From: googy2shoes@psnet.co.uk
To: hannahnutter@fastmail.com
Date: 22nd June
Subject: sleepover secrets.

Dear H,
I have the best news about that sleepover. Nesta and Lucy were so cool about it. They didn't tell anyone about me never snogging anyone. Nor did they say anything about Scott. All the boys were flirting with me as Nesta gave me a makeover! How's Luke? Hope he's good and still drop dead gorgeous. Hee, hee!

TJ
Miss ya loads.

Phillipa Franklin (12)
Matthew Arnold School, Oxford

An Alternative Chapter To 'Holes'
(In the style of Louis Sachar)

Stanley woke with a start.

It was the middle of the night. A chilled breeze blew around his shoulders. He lay thinking. Thinking about Zero. Thinking was he alive or ... or ... dead? He couldn't bear it any longer.

Stanley had been walking for miles. At least, that was what it felt like. The sun was just visible over the mountains ahead.

Back in his cot Stanley's idea of going to search for Zero had been great at the time. But now as the sun rose, it was getting hotter and hotter and Stanley's mouth was becoming drier and drier. His canteen was empty.

Suddenly Stanley felt faint and so he stopped to rest and catch his breath. As he looked around at his surroundings, the mountains in front caught his eye. He stopped and gazed. Something seemed familiar. Strangely familiar. He tried to think why. Then it came to him, his grandfather had sat on God's thumb. The mountain ahead had an oddly life-like fist poking out of its side!

'Argh!'

That was strange, thought Stanley; he could have sworn he just heard someone call out. *The heat must be playing with my mind,* he thought. But then as he got up to continue his journey he heard it again.

'Argh!' it cried. 'Help!'

Stanley ran quickly using all the energy he had left.

But then he stopped ...

There in the middle of a huge hole was Zero ...

... Surrounded by yellow spotted lizards!

Danielle Warren (13)
Matthew Arnold School, Oxford

The Bloody Werewolf

What was this strange phenomenon? What was happening to me? Well, I'll tell you …

As I started seeing hair growing on my palm, the hair was poking out like wires, my ears started feeling weird. I touched them, they felt like they were growing pointier and pointier, like a sharp knife. My nails they … they started getting sharper and pointier …

The next day I was feeling great but when I woke up …

Ahsan Hussain (14)
Matthew Arnold School, Oxford

Odysseus And The Cyclops

I can't believe what just happened to me. As I got closer to the noise of people screaming, I knew I was close to the Cyclops as I tried to sneak up to it because this huge monster had scared everyone away. But then the Cyclops saw me out the corner of his eye and then ... the Cyclops had seen me and grabbed me. He tried to eat me. Although his breath stank like a dustbin lorry.

I managed to get myself out of his grasp so I started to try and find my sword but it had happened to get attached to the Cyclops' loin cloth. I then found out that there was a rope right next to me in a bucket. I got an idea of tying it to make a lassoo to grab my sword. My idea had worked and me and the Cyclops started to exchange blows.

I then got a punch in and the Cyclops was staggering. I got him with my sword and the Cyclops was dead.

Jamie Cole (13)
Matthew Arnold School, Oxford

Hercules

I can't believe what happened to me today but I'm OK. Just hope it won't happen again but if I need to, I'll do it again. But this time I'll make sure he's dead!

It all started when I went to the jungle to have a little walk and I saw something. I wasn't too sure what it was but I saw it. It attacked me. I managed to fight it off me, when it started to walk away I saw that it was a lion!

This lion was as big as a ten-foot snake about to eat me! Not just eat me but eat me whole!

I carried on walking, thinking to myself, *I can't believe I fought that beast.* I thought I would barely make it alive with his big, gigantic mouth over me with his smelly breath blowing in my face! I thought *Hell! I'm going to die with his sharp claws in my chest feeling like a million pins sticking into me!* I thought, *I'll never live to tell the tale!*

The next day I was walking around in the village where I lived. Whilst I was walking I saw some people I had never seen before but they were after the lion that tried to kill me. The same lion had killed their friend and they were determined to find it, and make sure it was dead with 10 thousand dashes all over it as deep as a trench, with blood pouring out of it like a fountain. I'm glad I lived to tell this tale!

Jonnelle Jones (14)
Matthew Arnold School, Oxford

King Midas

I felt destroyed when I knew my life was over, all because my greed took over me.

It all began when I came across someone unexpectedly, and they granted me something I thought I could never have.

This witch gave me a power that I think everyone would like. I felt like the most powerful man alive.

This witch gave me the power to turn things into gold. I mean any little thing, into pure gold.

Later that day I tried my new powers out. I was like the man of gold. It wasn't until teatime my life was going to end. My wife and I were sat down ready to eat when I picked up my glass of wine ready to take a sip, when my glass turned to gold.

I didn't think anything of it until my food turned to gold as well. But did this mean I couldn't eat or drink again? I wasn't bothered about the need to eat.

Night had come and my belly was starving but I ignored it. My wife and I were getting ready for bed, but for me it was hard, everything I touched turned to gold.

I was heartbroken. I knew now I couldn't change my clothes or brush my teeth anymore. I got so upset I rushed to give my wife a hug and suddenly I had a gold statue in my arms where my wife was meant to be placed. I knew my life was over!

Rosie Kirkbride (14)
Matthew Arnold School, Oxford

The Golden Touch - King Midas

Oh my God, I can't believe what I've just done! I turned my wife into gold! I was the one that had wished that everything I touched should turn into gold, I had thought gold would brighten up my life, I thought my life would shine like a thousand diamonds, but no, my life's worse than being in a black hole.

I wish time would go back to just half an hour ago. So that I could take back my words, that everything I touch should not turn to gold, and that I hadn't touched my wife's smooth as silk arms and turned her into gold. But what should I do now? How do I get my wife back to being human?

Sadiya Bi (14)
Matthew Arnold School, Oxford

Alone

Hello, my name is Sebastian Hawthorn. The date is 3rd May 1917 and the time is around 8.15am right now.

My friend, Frank and I are in a dank and muddy trench. We're feeling homesick. Frank of his sister and I of my wife and children.

12.17pm

This is extremely hard to write. I've just received a letter. My wife, Jane, died of the flu last Wednesday. I hadn't heard from her for over 3 months, but I didn't know she was ill.

14.21pm

I can't keep my thoughts off Jane, but I must think of my country. It's deeply depressing here. Frank's keeping me laughing though.

16.14pm

Frank and I have been watching flying pieces of shrapnel and listening to repetitive gunfire all day. We've been talking about Jane and Frank's sister Molly and why we miss them.

17.56pm

Nobody wants to be here. Not even the men who weren't called up. They've seen the harsh reality of 'The Great War'. Not so great anymore! I ... wait, Frank's telling me that we've got some action? Here we go!

18.12pm

Frank's just been shot! No, this can't be happening. First my dearest Jane dead, now this. Wait! Frank's still alive!

18.19pm

Frank's dead. His hearty laugh and bright eyes all gone. Jane - her rich auburn hair and sweet smile all gone. I suppose that Leah and Martha, my daughters, are still alive, but where are they? Are they gone too? Goodbye cruel world!

Joe Harrison (12)
Matthew Arnold School, Oxford

A Day In The Life Of Nelson Mandela

6am

The keys rattled against my cell door, the same sound I had heard for the last 26 years. This was my normal wake-up call, it took me a few minutes to realise and then it hit me, it was my last day in prison.

6.30am

Breakfast was served, my normal bacon and egg was slid through my cell door hatch for the last time.

9am

Out for my daily exercise, a walk round the courtyard.

11am

I said goodbye to the other prisoners who I normally showered with, they all clapped and cheered and wished me all the best.

11.30am

I was escorted by the prison guards to see the warden who told me I was going to be released at 2 o'clock.

1pm

They brought me my suit, shirt and tie so I came out very smart.

1.50pm

They opened the cell door for the last time to take me to the main gate.

2pm

The gates opened, free at last. Waiting for me was Winnie, my wife, we hugged and kissed for the first time in 26 years. I couldn't believe the amount of people who had come to meet me, there were hundreds of my people plus newspaper, TV and radio presenters from all over the world.

7pm

We eventually arrived home and waiting for me were thousands of my own people.

11pm

Finally managed to get rid of the people outside my house so me and Winnie could be alone for the first time in 26 years.

Michael Younie (12)
Matthew Arnold School, Oxford

Stanley's Escape

Stanley decided to escape so he could go and find Zero because he was worried about him.

Stanley decided he would escape in the night while everyone was asleep and before he escaped he stole a rifle and a torch. He also took his canteen with him so he would survive in the desert.

During the night there was a convoy of army trucks and tanks and that's when he decided to escape. So he quietly climbed on the side of a tank with his rifle, torch and canteen that he had stolen.

After he escaped he went to look for Zero and somewhere to sleep where it was safe so he wouldn't die.

Josh Thorpe (13)
Matthew Arnold School, Oxford

The Creature

It was a dark, cold and petrifying night. Everywhere was pitch-black, all except this old house which had a fire burning brightly inside.

In that house was a creature so terrifying that no one, not even a ghost would go near.

It was Hallowe'en night, 567 years ago from that day and all the little kids were out trick or treating, all except one, Danny was waiting inside.

Tonight was the night that Danny was going to break into the old abandoned house and see what was inside. His mum had said that the creature that lived there died 567 years ago today and had been buried in St Horrors Cemetery, but he always came back on All Hallow's Eve to haunt us.

Danny did not believe in that old folks' tale.

So at 8pm Danny went out saying he was going trick or treating but walked straight to the big, old and creepy house. He walked very slowly up to the door and as he got there it creaked open. Danny stepped inside and the door slammed behind him, he was terrified.

He walked into the house more, he heard a noise from behind him, turned around and suddenly ... suddenly I can tell you no more.

Christina Simeone (13)
Matthew Arnold School, Oxford

Hercules

Hercules took Jason and the Argonauts on his quest to find the legendary and expensive golden fleece. This fleece could pick up gold from the river and make any man rich, it was the ultimate reward.

They searched for years and discovered its whereabouts in the island Crandor. It was guarded by the seven-headed hydra and if it was killed its teeth would drop out and grow into skeleton warriors. Then they would have to escape Neptune and return to Zeus and claim immortality.

They got onto the island, slayed the hydra and took the teeth before they grew and escaped the god Neptune.

Jack Preston (13)
Matthew Arnold School, Oxford

A Day In The Life Of A Dog

Goldie looked up. There was someone coming down the stairs. She stretched, stood up and through the door came ... Adam, her owner. She jumped up at him trying to lick his face.

'Down, come on, get off me!' he exclaimed.

Goldie wagged her tail madly but got down.

'Can I get my cup of coffee now?' he asked her.

Suddenly Goldie barked, there was someone else coming down the stairs. Goldie looked up.

'Hello Goldie!' It was Lara, Adam's wife. 'Come on Adam! Or we will be late for work!'

10 minutes later Goldie padded over to her water bowl. Adam and Lara had both gone to work. She began lapping up her water. She looked, listening. She had heard someone talking.

'Come on or they'll be back!' said the voice. Goldie trotted over to the door.

She growled. The door handle moved. She ran back behind the closet and waited.

'Come on let's see what's in here!'

As the door opened, Goldie bounded out barking madly.

'Argh! Help me!' screamed the robber as Goldie sank her teeth into his leg.

'Run!' yelled the other. But before they could move Goldie began barking wildly.

'What's going on in here?' Adam was back! He sprinted through the door staring at the two robbers. He grabbed the phone.

Later Goldie looked down at a bowl of food, she was wearing a new bravery rosette. *I could be a hero more often!* she thought.

Sophie Hutton (12)
Matthew Arnold School, Oxford

April Fool

Natalie was walking home, worrying about the next day. Today was the 31st March, nearly April Fool's Day. She had a reputation for fantastic pranks. She was worried because she hadn't come up with a single idea; her reputation was at stake.

She noticed a piece of paper on the floor that looked as if it had been ripped from a diary. Nosy by nature, she picked it up. It read;

'Dear Diary,
I've had the worst day ever. It was April Fools and everyone picked on me. There was one really mean prank.
It was all Graham's fault. He must have gone to school ultra early. He fixed it so that when I walked down the corridor I slipped on something slimy that wouldn't come off the back of my skirt and went skidding along. As I slid I pulled a string releasing a load of custard and Marmite-filled water balloons, so I am now drenched in the stuff. Then him and his mates poured a whole load of feathers over my head and they stuck because of the custard and Marmite. That's not all. They then picked me up, dragged me into the field, poured honey all over me and set me down on top of an ants' nest.
I am moving schools.
Anyway it's lights out now and I'm tired, I'll write more tomorrow.
Gina XXX'

Natalie put down the piece of paper and smiled, she'd had an idea!

Cathy Van Hear (12)
Matthew Arnold School, Oxford

Echo And Narcissus

Narcissus was the most handsome man in the whole of Greece, blond hair, hazel eyes; but unfortunately he thought he was too good for a goddess. Echo was a nymph, and as you know (because all nymphs are beautiful) she was very pretty.

During a peaceful walk through her beloved wood, Echo fell upon a clearing where Narcissus lay fanning herself. Echo was in love. She followed him everywhere. But she was unable to say anything to him!

Before Echo's finding of Narcissus she had been sent to talk to Hera (Zeus's wife) while Zeus was chasing other nymphs. Hera became very bored and suspicious and soon found out what was going on. She punished Echo by making her dumb, apart from repeating what others said.

Narcissus sent Echo away saying he knew what she wanted, and wouldn't marry her. Aphrodite (goddess of love) was most displeased at Narcissus' cruel words. With one swift, shimmering, silent dart, Aphrodite shot Narcissus with love. He looked down into the pool beside which he'd been lying, and saw his reflection. He wanted to touch the boy in the water, but every time he tried the boy disappeared. Narcissus had fallen in love with himself and wouldn't come away, so he withered to a flower that we still call Narcissus. Echo also withered away. But if you are in the hills and you shout out she will respond.

Hannah Robson (12)
Matthew Arnold School, Oxford

The Cockatrice

In an inn one day, a hooded figure leapt onto a table and cried, 'Good evening, friends! Look what I found!' He lifted up a small box.

'What is it?' asked a man.

'A cockatrice. I found it outside the inn.'

'Let's see.'

'You can't look at it! If anyone looks it in the eye, they'll be instantly turned to stone. I was nearly caught, myself! Fortunately, I have a mirror ...'

The door banged and an old man entered.

'Want to see a miracle?' started the hooded man.

'Just why I came! Show me.' There was silence as he used the mirror to look. He laughed, grabbed the box and tipped out the stuffed bird.

'There is your cockatrice! A trick, using the darkness inside the box and people's fear of seeing it clearly. Now leave, thief!'

He ran outside, then spotted a lizard nearby. A fly landed beside it. The lizard glanced at the insect, turning it to stone. He caught it at once, then re-entered the inn and shouted, 'Here is a *real* cockatrice! Come and take a look!'

Sighing, the old man took the box and peered inside, secretly closing his eyes as he did so. Emerging, he spoke, 'I fear your cockatrice is dead.'

'What? Impossible! Let me see that!' The furious man snatched his box and looked inside, immediately turning to stone.

'He must have found a basilisk,' explained the wise man, 'because of course, there is no such thing as a cockatrice.'

Sarah Montgomery (11)
Matthew Arnold School, Oxford

A Day In The Life Of Louisa Harding - A Victorian Child

It was September, one of the coldest days yet. I woke early. Edgar was lying sweetly in his cot, Mother was sobbing in the next room. That was usual, especially for Mother.

'Lou?' Hattie whispered from the shadows. I jumped. 'Yes?' I said, looking for her face in the darkness.

'It's today isn't it?' she said again, her voice wobbling.

'Go back to sleep Hattie, you shouldn't be awake now,' I said sternly. I went to her bed, kissed her gently and tucked her back in; the covers were damp with tears.

I turned to go back but her small hands gripped me tightly, 'No stay!' she said, she sounded frightened, her small face was covered with worry.

'Little Hattie!' I sighed. 'You'll wake Edgar up!' But I didn't mean it, I wanted to stay. I was every bit as frightened as she was but I had to be strong, for Hattie and for Mother.

We must have fallen asleep together as when I woke up I was lying with her, squashed as the small bed was barely big enough for Hattie. Mother came in, her eyes red like Hattie's had been. She was bustling around the room, finding every black piece of clothing she could. Edgar was crying softly in the background, it looked as if Mother didn't hear him or anything else for that matter. I got up; I was stiff and shaking, maybe with fear, maybe with the cold. It was my father's funeral.

Jenny Crosby (12)
Matthew Arnold School, Oxford

A Day Being Lindsay Lohan

My one wish has always been to be Lindsay Lohan, just for a day at least!

I laid in bed and warmth was in the air. Then I slept and that's all I can remember …

It must have been still early but my alarm clock was going off. I turned round and caught my eye in the mirror to find, wait a minute, as I looked in the mirror it wasn't me, it was … *Lindsay Lohan!*

I jumped out of bed and looked in my wardrobe and found some lush clothes, shoes and handbags in front of me. Then the phone went, I jumped onto my pink leather couch and picked it up. My face went red, I was going to The Brits and I was going in style! I picked out a red dress with matching shoes, diamond necklace, and my hair was wavy!

The limo picked me up at eight and life was great! The party was huge, everyone was there. I danced, talked, sang, it was by far the best party ever! You will never guess, Lemar came up to me and asked for my number and gave me a huge kiss!

Then out of nowhere, Dad was shouting and Mum was moaning, I turned around and unfortunately I was home again. I thought for a moment, *I want everything I did today but I want it for life, and no one is going to stand in my way! I'm going to make it happen!*

Tessa Hughes (12)
Matthew Arnold School, Oxford

Mystery

I have solved many mysteries in my time, but never have I come across one like this. It was a warm summer's night, but my candles were flickering. I was sat in my cold living room, smoking a cigar and reading today's newspaper, when I came across a strange article. It was about the Hinton's mansion. The family diamonds had been stolen. No sooner had I finished reading it, the phone rang. It was Knuckles. 'Hello Boss.'

'What is it now Knuckles?'

'Oh sorry Boss, the Hinton diamonds have been stolen!'

'Yes I know, I've just finished reading that.'

'Oh right, sorry Boss, they want you to solve the mystery.'

'Yes OK, I get the picture, I'll be down in a minute.'

I grabbed my coat, hat and pipe, then I picked my car keys up and left. To my great surprise it had started to rain. I got into my car and left the drive. It took me half an hour to get there.

Once I got to the crime scene I went to talk to John Hinton straight away. I got the full story off of him. There wasn't much information for me to get started on, but I managed to catch the thief in the end.

I went to interview the rest of the ... victims shall I say. The ex-butler Jim Boulder was telling me that the Hinton family were having a lot of money troubles.

Maariyah Razaq (14)
Matthew Arnold School, Oxford

Running

I ran. Not daring to look back in case he saw the hurt look in my eyes and the sorrowful tears streaming down. My feet dragged across the floor. Each step got harder and heavier whilst my heart thumped furiously against my chest. Gasping for breath I reached the door. With my shaking hands I desperately tried to open the door. Locked. The door was locked!

My head was throbbing as all the hurtful, hateful words screamed and yelled at me. I didn't want to believe what he said. But I had to. It was the truth and I had to accept it. Simply because ... because, that was the cruel, cold reality. I had to get away. I couldn't face him. It would tear me apart.

Quickly, I turned around. Ready to run faster than ever before, when suddenly I froze. Because there he was. Hovering hopelessly in front of me. A guilty look spread across his face as he glared at me. All I could feel was the pain. I felt sharp teeth penetrate my body, finding the freshest part of me and yanking it out. I could hear the crunching of my bones in its mouth and my blood trickling down its face. I instantly clutched my stomach to check I was still whole, and I was, even though I felt as if I had been torn apart and scattered about in a million pieces.

Hadia Mansour (13)
Matthew Arnold School, Oxford

Stix And The Chaos Knights

Once upon a time, in a faraway world, was the enchanted land. This land was home to all the fairies in the magical kingdom. The land had lush green grass, that felt like heavenly clouds underfoot. It smelt like toasted marshmallows, and you could almost taste the happiness. The sun shone all day and when it set, the sight was magical. The smooth, flowing sound of the legendary Omec waterfall, was so peaceful, it helped the fairies sleep at night.

But during a bright summer's afternoon, the enchanted land became a battlefield! The brutal Chaos Knights attacked! The fairies used all in their magic to defend their home, and almost used all the healing waters in the Omec waterfall, nevertheless, the Chaos Knights were too strong and overpowered the fairies!

Soon the putrid smell of dying fairies filled the air. Clear skies were replaced by dark storm clouds. The sight of havoc was unbearable, the cackle of Chaos Knights was dreadful and the atmosphere was so terrible you could almost taste the evil!

Only one fairy survived. His name was Stix. The future of the fairy kingdom lay in his hands. Stix had to fight for the land he had been brought up in. The enchanted land!

Stix was the last fairy in the magical world. He had large brown eyes and jet-black hair. Stix had strong fairy wings and a unique magical power. He had the power to call upon the elements; ferocious wind, mighty earth, rushing water and raging fire.

Tobias Warwick (13)
Matthew Arnold School, Oxford

Banished

A pair of eyes tracked a huge ship float out of orbit.

When it was gone, the body owning the eyes came out of the darkness, almost invisible with its jet-black hair and grey skin.

The man then walked through the valley stopping at every sound until he heard a footstep. He swivelled round, his cape with gold shoulder pads flying through the air.

A tranquilliser dart struck his face ...

When he came to a four-legged alien was there. It waved its green arm and spoke, 'You really should get some sleep ... what's your name?'

'Karross,' said the grey-skinned man, 'let me out!'

'No,' said the alien and introduced himself, 'I'm Zerlak.'

'Fine then,' Karross sighed. He swung his arm and broke the metal bars. Karross strolled to the exit.

'How?' exclaimed Zerlak.

'Bionic arm,' Karross replied as he went through the door.

'Wait!'

'What?'

'We need you for the assault.'

'Do they have ships there?'

'Yes.'

'When do we start?'

When Karross woke up the next day he was with an army of Zerlak's race.

'To the castle!' shouted Zerlak.

Karross ran behind them.

When he arrived the doors were down so he jumped past the fighting into a huge room. He found Zerlak dead on the floor. He turned to view the room - a huge creature jumped at him. Karross kicked the creature to the floor.

As he ran towards the hangar, he hoped there would be a ship capable of taking him home ...

Edmund O'Malley (12)
Matthew Arnold School, Oxford

A Day In The Life Of A Bee

That wonderful day being a bee. I was trying to work out how to use my wings. I felt my stomach, it was soft. It was covered with a fine layer of fuzz.

I managed to work out how to fly and I was off as if nothing was going to stop me.

I got outside and leant on a leaf. There was a green caterpillar inches away from me. It made a chewing noise. It was eating the leaf I was on. From close up caterpillars are really ugly and before I knew it it was getting dark.

I found a nice bed of grass and fell asleep and in the morning I was back to normal.

Alicia Hulewicz (11)
Matthew Arnold School, Oxford

A Day In The Life Of A Soldier In A Trench

I woke up this morning to find myself up to my knees in horrible, mucky water, with rats all over me. I had breakfast with my comrades, a tin of corned beef. I didn't particularly like it, but it was the best the army could afford to give us, but I'd gotten used to it now.

Then, I heard a splash; something had fallen into the water ... there was a loud bang. Before I could work out what was going on I saw one of my comrades lying on the ground, mortally wounded, screaming in agony! I reached for my gun, loaded it, then climbed out of the trench. A Nazi suddenly came out of nowhere and stabbed me in the back, I reached for my pistol and shot him in the neck, he died before he hit the floor.

I was bleeding badly; searching desperately for the squad's medic. I found him in a large puddle, face down, dead. I thought there was no hope for me now. I took his sub-machine gun from him and climbed the wall of the trench.

I saw a group of Nazi soldiers, they couldn't see me so I crept up on them. I gunned my way through. I got shot in the leg in the process and my gun ran out of ammo. I lost consciousness.

I awoke four days later in hospital. My leg was in pain. That was my last day in the trenches.

George Newson (13)
Matthew Arnold School, Oxford

Friday 13th

On Friday 13th there was a man called Ed that was running late for a very important job interview. This day was a very unlucky day for most people, but especially Ed. 'Why do I have to have an important job interview on this day, why me?' Ed gasped in fear. He got changed rushed downstairs and had a really quick breakfast. Ed had just bought a second-hand car from Cruise Cars. After he had his breakfast, he ran outside, not forgetting his car keys, and got into his second-hand Ford Focus that was a greasy green colour, but Ed obviously liked it.

He started his car and drove off to his job interview an hour and 15 minutes late. About halfway there it started to heavily rain. Ed had no choice but to turn his windscreen wipers on. As soon as he did they were screeching really badly. The screeching of them really annoyed him. *Screech! Screech! Screech!* It annoyed him so much that he had to stop his screen wipers. It was raining so heavily that he couldn't see through his windows. As he was driving along, rain splattered and splattered all over the windows. *Crash! Bang!* 'Argh! I'm going to sue Cruise Cars.'

Bang! No one heard from Ed since that day.

Aiya Jibali (13)
Matthew Arnold School, Oxford

The Robots Have Lost It

Last night we had reports that an army of robots had gone crazy and had formed an army which was terrorising America. These so-called 'helpful' robots are forcing their way through Los Angeles and they show no mercy. US troops are trying to hold them back, but they cannot do so on their own. The US are asking other countries to come and help in the fight against the robots.

The robots were made in the Akrobot laboratory which is in the Nevada desert. Head scientist, Dr Robert Wolf, had this to say. 'The robots are controlled by a chip in the middle of their chest. If the chip is taken out, they will cease to operate.'

So far the death toll is 16,686 people. This might not sound like many compared to the population of the US, but of course it is. The place worst hit by the robots is Las Vegas, which is now under their control. As we speak, the United Kingdom is sending in all their troops in one large force.

The robots' arms can change into machine guns. However, fortunately they have limited ammunition. The robots were designed to help mankind and to make our lives better. However, they are making life much worse. The latest news is that the air force of the UK has destroyed most of the robots in Las Vegas.

Tom Peacock (13)
Matthew Arnold School, Oxford

Mistakes

It was never meant to happen.

When I was younger, I thought my life was going to be perfect. That was then. Now I am prisoner to a monstrous whirlpool, plunged in head-first. Everywhere I turn people resent me for what I am, making discriminating judgement before taking a proper look at me, inside. Despite this, I could get through, if only ... the father would merely consider supporting me.

A ray of sunshine, a fresh start, a glimmer of hope. Isn't that what a baby was supposed to be? To me, it's nothing, an abyss, a time bomb. I feel nothing for it, yet it's my own flesh and blood, and worst of all, I'm its only hope.

My thoughts were disturbed as Dad stormed through the door.

'We need to talk.'

When I saw the antagonised grimace on Dad's face, fury welled up inside me.

'We are all behind you on this, we can sort it out, let you focus on your GCSEs.'

My emotions turned from fury to bitterness. 'Is that what you think? That I can murder it and just forget about it?'

He couldn't have hurt me more. The way he said it made it all the more devastatingly true. This was my life now, wasn't it? My heart cracked and I split in two. I stumbled out of the room, scarcely making it to the bathroom, before my stomach seized up. Then came the bleeding. I was punched in the stomach again. I keeled over.

It isn't fair.

No ...

Stop ...

It was never meant to happen.

Sabrina Gardner (13)
Matthew Arnold School, Oxford

Perseus And Medusa

I had just defeated the unbeatable beast Medusa. I had stopped the Greek murdering monster from killing again.

I barely made it out alive, but I made it. I survived. It all began when an old beggar man rushed out of the cave frantically, and screamed 'Help! Help! There is a monster in the cave, and it has turned my friends to stone. It's huge. It's as big as a temple tower, with snakes like wire for hair.'

I crept into the cave, the overwhelming stench hit me like a ton of bricks, I climbed over damp, slippery rocks, all I could see was my breath in the cold air, and all I could hear was my heart pounding, as if it was going to jump out my chest. In the distance all I could hear was the hideous hissing and demented, cackling laughter of the monster Medusa.

Creeping towards this terrifying beast, I held my shining silver shield by my side ready to block her glare. I screamed her name, tricking her to look at my shield, my plan had worked, in an instance of her looking into my shield, she screeched an agonising scream, and right in front of my eyes, she turned to stone.

Max Bolton (14)
Matthew Arnold School, Oxford

George And The Dragon

I can't believe what I've just done. I never thought I could have achieved it. I fought the dragon with my mighty, heavy sword. My arm was aching but I knew I had to keep on fighting. As I struck him with my sword, he began to make a dreadful whining noise, as he fell to the ground. As he hit the ground, it shook like a terrible earthquake beneath my feet.

As I stood back to look at what I had done, I felt proud. There was just this giant lump laid out, cold on the floor. I had saved lives from being taken by the unbeatable beast. I have saved the town from terrible frustration and from the horrid dragon. Thank God that I am still alive to tell the tale.

Elizabeth Webb (14)
Matthew Arnold School, Oxford

The Enchanted Forest

Once upon a time there was believed to be an enchanted forest, deep in the heart of Middletonne. If you are lucky enough to get a few yards in, you can smell the stench of the magical mushrooms within, which make you feel all happy inside. People believe that if you listen close enough you can hear the wind calling your name. If you get in far enough you can taste the sweetness in the air above you. If you get into the heart of the forest, you can hear the sound of the heartbeat of the evil creature underneath.

One day Quintinus and Hoblong were walking through the forest when they heard thunderous footsteps behind them, and they thought to themselves, *Bailey*.

James Dallimore (13)
Matthew Arnold School, Oxford

Lard Wars

A long time ago, in a galaxy not far away ...

Puke Skykiller, the fiercest Gedi in the whole universe, was riding on the Century tiger (the fastest spacecraft in the universe) with his trustful friends, Pan Mole and Princess Fear. Suddenly the ship quaked.

'Our ship has turned on the hyper-drive and the autopilot,' Pan said.

'Well turn it off then!' Princess Fear shouted.

'I can't,' replied Pan.

'We're heading to the cloud planet Nestin.'

The ship landed on a platform. Puke felt fear.

'Get off my hand Puke,' Princess Fear moaned.

'Look over there, the army of the king, Suntroopers!' Pan cried while taking his pistol out.

Both Fear and Pan were shooting the orange-coloured spacemen. But in the distance Puke saw something ... Darth Larder, the most feared person in the galaxy. Puke turned on his baguette-saber ready for battle.

They fought a terrifying battle lasting around 5 minutes, but Puke's baguette-saber was cut in half by Larder.

'Now Puke, I must tell you the truth ... Bacon will make you fat.'

'Nooooo!'

Gary Rawlings (12)
Matthew Arnold School, Oxford

The Spider And The Swamp

One cold, damp day a small boy called James got out of bed and shivered. He could see his breath in front of him. He reached and took his dressing gown from the door, but as soon as he took it off, the doorknob tried to bite him.

He slipped out of his room and down to his parents' room. They were gone. In their place was a green slimy mess. Suddenly the floor gave way and he heard a piercing scream. His sister was half eaten in a huge spider's mouth. She was screaming and then she was gone.

A bigger spider ate the smaller one just as it was advancing on a horror-struck James. James ran, he looked back and saw a green slime where the spider had been.

James kept running. He slipped and fell into a huge swamp where he sank. Something wet went past his feet. Something was breathing in his ear.

'James, get up, you'll be late,' his mother was calling.

James opened his eyes. His dog George was breathing in his ear and licking his feet. 'Oh George!' said James, as his sister Carmen came into his room.

Amy Grant (12)
Matthew Arnold School, Oxford

The Living Droids

On a planet a long way away, above an old forest, a storm was brewing. The first shower droplets, another roll of thunder, the rain increased. Around an almost non-existent camp were droids, two-legged and tripods. Nothing moved nor stirred. The rain patted down on the machine's battered and twisted plates.

Suddenly a bolt of lightning hit one of the droids, with the smell of melting plastic and circuitry. More bolts shot out of the first droid, hitting others then it stopped. Then something moved. With a groan the droids slowly uprighted themselves. There was a minute of silence as they ran diagnostics.

'Who are we?' said a droid commander. He was two-footed.

'I don't know, but I know you are the commander,' said one.

There were seven of them - two three-legged and five two-legged.

'Sir, come and look at this,' one said.

The commander who had called himself '1' came over. It was a ship, the size of a house. As he touched it a hatch opened. A laser bolt flamed into the ground.

'Get in,' ordered 1.

They ran inside. 2 and 3 found the guns. They went into capsules marked gun control. They then connected computer leads to nodes on their waists. Then they seemed to stop moving but now only controlled the guns' turrets. They started firing.

Oliver Crosbie-Higgs (12)
Matthew Arnold School, Oxford

The Legend Of Gelert

A thirteenth century Prince of North Wales whose name was Llewelyn, had a palace at Beddgelert.

One day he went out hunting, leaving his trusty dog Gelert to guard his baby son. When he returned Llewelyn was greeted by a joyful Gelert; only he was covered in blood. Llewelyn suddenly worried about his child's safety and hastened to find him.

However, when Llewelyn reached his child's room, he found the cot empty and the floor stained with blood. Expecting the worst, Llewelyn plunged his sword into Gelert's side only to find the poor dog's dying cry was answered by a baby crying.

Lleweyln searched and searched and finally discovered his heir, alive. Lying next to him was the carcass of a great wolf, which Gelert had slain. Llewelyn was devastated, he was said never to have smiled again.

The place where Gelert lies is named 'Beddgelert' or 'Gelert's Grave'.

Olivia Sharp (12)
Matthew Arnold School, Oxford

An Alternative Chapter To Stanley's Escape In Holes
(In the style of Louis Sachar)

On July 17th 1998 Stanley Yelnats became only the second ever boy to even try and escape Camp Green Lake juvenile detention centre.

Zero hadn't returned. All through the hot day Stanley had thought he should go and find him. But he didn't. He thought he should fill his canteen and sneak away. But he didn't. He thought he should at least make sure Zero's records weren't destroyed. But he didn't.

Hearing the water truck approaching, Stanley merely stepped out of his hole. The boys hadn't helped him with Zero's hole; but then again he didn't expect them to. Mr Pendanski served Armpit, X-ray and the others. When he came to Stanley, he waited as if he didn't want anyone to hear him say, 'Go round and get this, then jump in. The keys are in it.'

Stanley was confused as Mr Pendanski kicked the canteen under the truck and shooed him. Stanley took a while to realise what was going on, but ran around the truck, and jumped in ...

The keys were in the ignition as Mr Pendanski had promised. Stanley tried, but the truck wouldn't budge.

Scratch, scccrattch.

Mr Sir heard the engine starting with a bang and was sprinting towards Stanley. The truck still wouldn't move.

Scccrattch.

'Use the gear stick!' screamed Mr Pendanski.

Mr Sir was approaching all too quickly, when the gears slid with a screech to first ... second ... and third ...

As the truck rumbled away, Mr Sir shot ... and missed.

James Logan (12)
Matthew Arnold School, Oxford

Theseus And The Minotaur

I can't believe what I have just seen. How could such a beast be living on this Earth? I didn't think I could do it. I did. I just killed a Minotaur.

It started when I was sneaking through a giant stone maze, the walls were stained with blood and there were hundreds of human bones on the floor. They were crunching and cracking under each step I took.

I could tell that I was getting near the beast because the stench was horrendous, it smelt like decaying skin. I could almost taste it. By this time my heart was beating faster than ever.

As I turned and entered the centre of the maze, the monster was devouring a fresh human body. It was finished in a matter of minutes. It stood up. It was 7ft tall, it had a human body with muscles like marbles and a bull's head twice the size of normal. Fresh blood was dripping from its lips. My sword kept slipping out of my sweaty hands. I took a swipe at it. It was driving me backwards, my sword was screeching and sparks were flying as it bashed against the stone wall.

I was getting furious. My sword was slicing through the icy air like a knife through warm butter. With one last swipe I chopped off the monster's head. It landed with a thud on the floor and its body fell into a heap. That is my story of how I killed the mighty beast.

Kieran Tiller (14)
Matthew Arnold School, Oxford

Theseus And The Minotaur

Oh my God! My children have been killed. Their flesh was on the mud walls, also on the floor. I felt so sad, as if my future had been taken away. I was on my knees crying when a Greek guardian told me that it was a half man, half beast that had killed my children. I rushed through the bamboo, then stormed through the confusing maze.

There it was, the monster of my children. The vile beast that tore them from part to part. The stench was like rotting meat, that stench was my children. My eyes opened up with rage. My sword sharpened like a gladiator's cage. The horns of the horrifying beast were as hideous as a scruffy horse's hooves.

I have struggled through the labyrinth, through traps, through the impossible. The Minotaur charged at me. I had no choice but to charge. I could not stop my rage for my children, just could not stop.

My sword snapped into the beast's hairy chest. It did not give in, nor did I. I charged with what was left of my sword. Suddenly I fell into the one-foot long fist. I bled, bled and bled out of my nose but I still fought. With a strain I chucked my sword and it hit the heart of the beast.

I had done the impossible that no one had ever done before. My eyes could not believe it. *Argghhh!* The Minotaur collapsed, *thump* went the floor. Revenge was complete.

Adil Hussain (13)
Matthew Arnold School, Oxford

Theseus And The Minotaur

All I could smell was rotting flesh, there were rotten remains covering the cold concrete floor. My hands were shaking. I was terrified.

I turned to the sixth corner to find a huge, horrifying beast devouring human remains. I panicked. I was about to turn back and run but the beast had spotted me.

It looked even more hideous than it smelt. It had a bull's body but stood on two legs like a human. It had short, brown, ragged hair smothered in human guts and remains. It had enormous horns either side of its large beastly head.

I was shaking more than ever now. The large creature with its bull-like features moved towards me. I took a few steps back, then stopped and realised I hadn't come to see the Minotaur, but I had come to defeat the dangerous beast.

I drew my sword from my carry case. 'Feeshe!'

Roar! Roar! The beast pulled its large feet away from the human remains, showed its claws and charged towards me. I stuck my sword out in front of me and closed my eyes in fear. The beast ran straight towards my sword like a bull in a bullring. My sword went straight into the beast's heart.

Aaahroar! The beast roared. I opened my eyes in amazement. The beast fell to the floor with a large *crash!* I ran out, out of the labyrinth to find safety. Then I came to you and told you my story.

Samantha Hobbs (14)
Matthew Arnold School, Oxford

George And The Dragon

I remember the day I was truly amazed with myself, reason being that I destroyed that deadly dragon.

I didn't believe I could achieve this. It was outstandingly frightening and very loud. I can remember the point when it kicked me over like a ragdoll and I was equipped with no other weapon except my dagger which was in my sock.

I ripped it out without a second to waste and pounced at the dragon like a furious tiger and continuously jabbed it into the dragon's eye. I watched the dragon scream and bleed in a pool of blood.

Ashley Creed (14)
Matthew Arnold School, Oxford

Daedalus And Icarus

I'm free. Alive with great feelings. Just free and proud. I can feel the hot breeze against my face. No! Now I am getting worried. My son gets closer and closer to the sun. 'Stop!' I shout but he is too far away to hear me. I feel a drop of hot honey on my head.

Then it happens, my son falls to his death with a loud scream. He shouts, 'Dad!' but it is too late.

Only a few moments ago he flew as perfectly as a bird only to then drop like a stone seconds later. The devastating sound of my son's screams as he fell to his death keep spinning in my head. The sound drowns my thoughts.

I am now up on the hilltop. My son's body is swarmed with people like a plague of locusts. I felt that it was my fault; my son's life coming to an end. Had I not taught him right? Was it my fault that he was so foolish? That the could fly so close to the sun that he could fall ferociously and plummet to his death?

Well, that's how it all happened and how my son is no more.

Robert Tyreman (13)
Matthew Arnold School, Oxford

An Alternative Chapter To 'Holes'
(In the style of Louis Sachar)

Stanley had a plan.

Finally.

He had been awake all night, trying to figure out how he would escape and rescue Zero, and now he knew what to do. But he didn't know how he would manage it.

That day, as he was digging his hole, he gave his plan some careful thought. His plan was this:

He would wake up in the middle of the night.

But he didn't have an alarm clock.

He would sneak past the counsellor guarding the dormitory.

But he didn't know how.

He would run to the water truck and start the engine.

But he didn't have the key.

He would drive into the desert and find Zero.

But he didn't know how to drive.

That was some plan, wasn't it?

Stanley changed his plan. Instead of waking up in the middle of the night, why didn't he just wait until everyone else was asleep?

Then he thought.

His shovel!

If he dug really quietly he could escape the dormitory, but the lock on the truck.

As Mr Sir turned round to jump back on the truck, there was a noise and something fell out of his pocket.

A penknife.

Just as Stanley was about to give it back to Mr Sir, he changed his mind.

He pocketed it.

It might just be useful for picking the lock on the truck door, he decided.

Later that night, as he lay in bed, thinking it all over, he realised he had a foolproof plan.

Or so he thought.

Polly Dunsmore (12)
Matthew Arnold School, Oxford

Escape From Camp Green Lake
(In the style of Louis Sachar)

The day Stanley escaped was the hottest yet. He left at 5.20, just before the others woke up. He crept to the shovel shed.

It was still very hot and muggy.

The breakfast was already out, fortunately for him.

The shovel shed was open, fortunately for him.

Mr Sir was awake, unfortunately for him.

He grabbed a shovel.

X-ray's shovel.

He ran as fast as his short, fat and stubby legs would carry him. As he was running he fell into a large hole, bumping his arm on the way down. He had bumped it on a large white wooden plank.

Unless it was what he thought it was.

It seemed to be some kind of door. He managed to wrench it open with his shovel. Inside, it was like some kind of house. It had many rooms, but a percentage of them were full of yellow spotted lizards.

They were the only rooms that were not full of onions ...

He found a book on the floor, saying, 'Charles Walker'.

A school book.

Stanley slept in one of the rest rooms which was also full of coal and scruffy old manuals.

Boat manuals.

This was Charles Walker's boat.

It took Stanley at least five days to dig the top of the boat out. He was living on mouldy water and onions. The lizards kept away from Stanley. *Was it the onions?* he thought.

When he finally dug it out, he stared into the emptiness. In the distance he saw a small figure walking towards him ...

Georgia Fogden (12)
Matthew Arnold School, Oxford

Escape From Camp Green Lake
(In the style of Louis Sachar)

When Stanley escaped it was the hottest yet.

Stanley woke up this morning feeling energetic and strong. As usual, the other boys were up. Mr Sir wasn't up yet.

While the boys sat waiting, Zero said, 'Maybe we can escape.'

'You're mad,' shouted X-ray.

'Well maybe we could if you think about it,' replied Zero.

'You're mad!' shouted X-ray again.

'Zero is right, there is a way,' said Stanley, 'you see outside it's misty.'

The boys packed themselves ready for a long journey. As they were walking, they heard a thunderous drop on the floor, X-ray had fainted.

Stanley carried X-ray until he was strong enough. They could see God's Thumb in sight. A tall mountain.

Night-time fell. The boys took a rest. When they woke, they thought that they would be back where they began.

Stanley and the other boys were walking, they came to a road.

Armpit said, 'Why don't we flag down a car?'

'Guys, guys, it's me mum, me mum,' shouted Stanley with joy.

The police arrived, Stanley was saved. 'It's alright son, we know you're innocent.'

The boys lived happily. Meanwhile Camp Green Lake was closed.

Rachel Gibbs (13)
Matthew Arnold School, Oxford

Theseus And The Minotaur

What's that smell? What's that noise? What or who's there?

'Show yourself,' I ordered nervously. A breath of cold air flew past me. It made the hair on the back of my neck stand on end like the quills on a porcupine's back. Then a bellowing growl forced itself into my ears. A stream of steam came creeping round the corner, a pitch-black silhouette followed. I could hear footsteps. If you could call ground-shaking thuds that. They got louder and closer. I then saw a pair of hooves fly past my head, narrowly missing my nose, as the beast reared.

It was the Minotaur! Eyes like a red-hot furnace, full of hatred and evil. Its horns sharp and ready.

It landed on the floor, the ground shook, then moved into its charge position, steam puffing out of its nostrils. Its hoof scraping the floor.

I was about to turn and run, when I remembered why I was here. I pulled my sword out of its scabbard and raised my shield. It charged at me, so I charged back. I was about to stare death in the face.

James Walsh (13)
Matthew Arnold School, Oxford

Pandora's Box

Why was I so stupid? I have given the world a great hateful future. Why couldn't I have just got on with my life instead of opening that box of evil?

As the box was given to me, I felt a presence run through me as I held the box, and then as I put it down a great warmth sailed through the room. I had to open it. I was told it was full of hatred and death, and showed the future of the world. So I did.

Then as I unlocked the box, the lid swung open and a great suction engulfed the room and great screams ran loose. I saw inside the box red clouds, and souls surrounded me. I tried to shut the box but the vacuum was too strong. The souls in the box blew through the room and sent a great chill changing up my back.

Finally they left me and my house, and spread through the town. I felt so guilty. Then, in the bottom of the box, I saw a little yellow glow of hope. It was hope. There was hope.

James Kaye (13)
Matthew Arnold School, Oxford

Escape From Camp Green Lake
(Written in the style of Louis Sachar)

The day Stanley escaped was the hottest yet.

The sun was beating down on the dry lake bed. Stanley could feel the sweat dripping down his face.

The rest of the group of boys were busily trying to get heir holes finished.

Stanley looked up to see a shadow approaching his hole. It was X-ray, towering down on Stanley, glaring at him.

Stanley only had one thing on his mind at that point, and that was getting out. Running out. Escaping, out of the camp.

Just then he thought of the perfect opportunity.

Stanley spun round, quickly.

Reached for his shovel, quickly.

Got out of his hole, quickly, and smacked X-ray round the face so powerfully that he fell to he ground. Stanley had no reason to do this but it felt good.

Stanley dropped his shovel and ran.

He ran so quickly that he soon got out of breath. He sat down behind a dirt pile, but couldn't stay for long as he saw a huge dust cloud building on the horizon.

He knew it would be the warden with Mr Sir but he didn't care.

Stanley shuddered as he heard the far-off whisper of the warden softly speaking, 'Excuse me?'

Stanley stood up and ran as fast as he could for as long as he could.

Then he fell.

Martha Howells (13)
Matthew Arnold School, Oxford

King Arthur

I can't believe it's true ... As I stepped forward out of the early morning mist the crowd parted to let me pass, a few of the crowd gave me encouragement, but most just stared as I walked past.

The first thing I saw was the stone with the great glinting sword shining in the little morning light. I stepped forward, every step a huge weight on my feet. The walk felt like a mile, and with every beat of my pounding heart I drew closer to the sword.

Finally I reached the stone and my breath caught in my throat. I felt hundreds of pairs of eyes on the back of my neck. I grasped the sword with both hands. I could feel its smooth cold metal on my hot skin. I felt a great surge of electrifying energy course through my hands and explode down the hilt of the sword. My whole body shook as I slowly but surely lifted the great sword from its resting place.

As I lifted it into the air it seemed as if a spell was broken and everybody began to cheer. The sun seemed to be rejoicing as well, as a shard of light flew down and shattered on the brilliant blade. And then came the chanting, 'King Arthur! King Arthur!'

Nicholas Salmon (13)
Matthew Arnold School, Oxford

Escape From Camp Green Lake
(In the style of Louis Sachar)

The day Stanley escaped from Camp Green Lake was the hottest yet. On the day he escaped Stanley was feeling nervous about whether he would make it or not, live or die all on his own.

He nicked pickled onions from the warden's fridge and the shovel from his hole.

He got going. Everyone was having dinner so they couldn't see him.

He was worried.

He was nervous about whether he would make it.

He had been planning this for weeks now.

He got quite far and was getting tired but dug a hole. It was bigger lengthways and wider than him in width so it just fitted. He didn't want people at Camp Green Lake seeing him in the distance because it would look like a big ridge in the ground. He woke up the next day and for breakfast he had picked onions.

He was worried.

He was nervous about whether he would make it.

When he was getting ready to go he saw a yellow spotted lizard in his hole on his pickle jar.

He reached down to get the jar, sweating. He knew he was probably going to die anyway.

Robert Hainge (13)
Matthew Arnold School, Oxford

George Fights The Dragon

The fire ripped through the clouds. The dragon swooped down again. His claw caught the back of my neck, making a massive gash that immediately started to pour with blood. I dived to the rocky floor and took cover behind a boulder of rock. But before I knew it the creature was down on me again, thrashing at me with his majestic claws and pelting the occasional fire ball.

I ducked out from behind the rock and pulled out a sharp five-inch flint from my belt. Now I was poised and prepared for action. The dragon swooped down like a swallow so his feet scraped along the ground, causing rocks and pebbles to fly everywhere. This was my chance. As it drew ever nearer I braced myself for the impact.

It reached me and I jumped with all my might. I latched onto the side of its scaly green body and hauled myself onto its back so I was riding it. With the flint in my hand I lunged at its head and buried the flint into its skull. The creature roared and tried to lash out but it couldn't reach me. Then I pulled out a second flint and plunged it into the eye of the dragon. It roared again and spiralled down blinded, plummeting to the ground.

I jumped just at the right moment, and turned to see the dragon smash into the floor, killed.

Sam Trinder (12)
Matthew Arnold School, Oxford

The Loch Ness Monster

I stopped the boat, I looked across the lake at the bubbles. I moved slowly towards the bubbles, holding my camera tightly. I looked into the water, then, suddenly a huge snake-like monster violently emerged out of the lake. I quickly jumped from my boat and swam to safety. I watched my boat being smashed to pieces by this monstrous creature. Then I suddenly thought, *my camera!* I quickly grabbed it from the ground and held it up, the creature had gone.

I swam towards the wreck of my boat and hauled myself onto a piece of wood. I looked into the deep, I could see a faint shadow beneath me. I watched the tape over and over again, noticing its snake and almost dragon-like features. I had seen nothing like its green scaly skin and its big black eyes. I couldn't believe I'd just witnessed the Loch Ness monster emerging from the lake.

I have been to the lake a number of times since, now and again I see a dark shadow beneath me, but it's about as normal to me now as a bird flying. I don't take my camera anymore, the villagers are trying to hunt the monster down, I see them firing bullets into the lake and dumping nets in hope of capturing the monster. That's something I don't want.

Lauren Gayton (11)
Matthew Arnold School, Oxford

The Disaster Of Icarus And Daedalus

Icarus soared. He laughed as the cold breeze rushed past him. As he turned round he saw his father taking off and breathed a sigh of relief. They were almost there.

Daedalus held his breath and jumped. Half expecting to find himself falling, he opened his eyes and breathed in the sickly scent of the honey and feather wings. He noticed Icarus a way ahead and gracefully moving his arms. He started to catch up. Suddenly something tugged on Daedalus' mind. He watched Icarus and suddenly realised how high he was flying. However, Daedalus didn't mind, he saw the cloudy sky, forgot about it and smiled to see his son flying so proudly. Suddenly the sun dazzled Daedalus' eyes. The sun had come up and the burning heat tore through Daedalus' mind. He thought about his son and how high he was. He screamed.

Something flicked onto Icarus' hand, he looked down and his eyes widened to see the dry honey in its liquid form; something else brushed past Icarus' arm. It was a single feather.

Daedalus watched his son's arms flailing in the wind. Again he cried out and started flapping his arms to try and reach Icarus, but he was too far ahead. Daedalus watched feathers and melted honey fall from Icarus. He cried. Finally the last feather fell and Icarus dropped. Daedalus' screams mingled with the birds' calls like a huge symphony of despair. However, all sound stopped as Icarus splashed into the water below. He was gone.

Peter Endicott (12)
Matthew Arnold School, Oxford

Robin Hood

This was the big moment. I was climbing the high tower to King John's chamber. *Little John should have got to the prisoners by now,* I thought, sweating all over. I just managed to get up the cold, stone wall of the tower and flip myself through the window.

There slept the king, his bags of gold scattered around him. I drew my bow and carefully sent a long rope and arrow through the prison chamber window, towards Little John and the prisoners.

One by one, King John's riches went down the rope and, as the last bags went down, I spotted the prisoners escaping past the sleeping sheriff.

But unfortunately, as I began my victory escape, one bag dropped. The king awoke immediately and cried, 'My gold! Robin Hood! Guards, seize him!'

At once, guards from all over the castle came running through the gates. Arrows came soaring in from all angles. I let out a cry of disbelief as the drawbridge came thundering down on me. I had nowhere else to go. I felt like a mouse caught in the clutches of a cat.

I scampered up the wall and through a window. I gasped. The sheriff was standing with a flame torch. He swung it at me and caught the curtains, setting them on fire. I ran past him, heart thundering, and climbed on the roof. I had nothing to lose. I leapt, straight into the bottomless river.

Robin Smith (11)
Matthew Arnold School, Oxford

Atlantis Submerged

I exploded out of my bottomless sleep. Dark, rumbles of death, could be heard throughout the house. Possessions of mine shattered. I panicked; what was happening?

I dashed down the rickety, mud-laden stairs. From the outside I heard a blast of bellowing. The forest aroma smelt of fresh gorgeous life. Water gushed around my feet urging me to plunge and get swept away. My brother Icarus stood waving impatiently, he pointed.

Ahead a huge mass of white horses galloped ferociously towards my bulk. They called whinnying in a crash of waves. Still the water crept upwards soaking my life and world away. The trees told me to run, their blossoming leaves hypnotised my body. The adrenaline kept my spirit going. A dozen screams and shrieks filled my skull.

Next to me glided an individual. Was this Hades coming to use my soul or was it my imagination? I glanced onwards the sky was blocked out by the waves.

Slipping, sliding my carcass went into spasms. Falling, my body went limp. The water gurgled, screeched and snarled over me. My life was walking towards the exit as my eyes closed in bitter terror. *Is this the end?* I thought as the poison pulled and moaned at me.

A soft, warm, tender hand reached out, bubbles fled from my mouth. The wave had arrived. The world had gone black like the stark, black night, as the long winding river of death took me downstream.

Daniel Saxton (12)
Matthew Arnold School, Oxford

King Midas And The Golden Butterfly

By all the gods of Olympus, what have I asked for? I only ever meant the best ... well, I was greedy. Greedy wishes never work. If only I had been more careful ...

But no, I wished for the Golden Touch. I can't take it back. And to think it all started with one tiny butterfly ... yes, I remember. I saw the beautiful butterfly as it morphed into flying gold in the setting sun. And I wanted gold forever and ever ... I never thought I'd get my wish.

The next night I saw the butterfly again. I hadn't yet realised that my wish was granted. I saw the butterfly and wanted to catch it for my beloved daughter, so she could see its magical transformation. But as I caught it, it turned to gold. Metal gold.

I was amazed and joyful. It was gold forever. But it was cold and lifeless as a stone. It had lost that mysterious, translucent air that had made it so lovely.

I let it slip through my fingers. It fell for what seemed like hours until it hit a rock and slowly shattered into a thousand golden shards.

The rays of sunset began to glimmer in gold as they had before. But the butterfly had lost its magic. Forever.

As I realised what a horrible thing I had done, I wept. My daughter came and hugged me. And her loving arms turned to gold, and she was lost.

Kelly Kochanski (11)
Matthew Arnold School, Oxford

Theseus And The Minotaur

I was ready. I trudged through the piles of dirty, dead rotting bodies. I looked up and got my first glimpse of the beast.

It vanished out of my sight, so I walked cautiously to where it had been standing and looked around. It jumped at me aggressively and slashed across my face. Its claws were like little razors ripping into my skin. I immediately got up and drew my sword.

The Minotaur roared loudly in my direction. I slashed its neck and blood gushed out like water from a fountain. It struck me again. In a sharp movement I stabbed it in the gut then jumped on its back.

It swayed from side to side in an attempt to throw me off. I impaled its back with my sword and gripped onto it tight so as not to fall off. Then it stopped moving.

I walked up to its head, but it caught me off guard and chucked me effortlessly into an alcove of dead bodies. It then threw a punch towards me and I dodged it quickly. It threw another punch as I reached for a steel chain by my side and swiped it with it. Then within a split second I jumped on its back, gathered my sword and hacked away at its horn.

The Minotaur screamed a final cry for help. But by then I had stabbed it with the horn, victory!

Mike Whillock (12)
Matthew Arnold School, Oxford

Achilles, The Trojan Horse

It was dark and dingy. We sat in silence, cramped and damp. We couldn't move. We didn't dare move. If we did we'd be shredded meat. All I could smell was my soldiers' sweat and their blooded swords. I could see nothing. 'Let's move,' I whispered. I lifted the trapdoor. Moonlight flooded in revealing the silent, sleeping Trojans. Their jugs of wine spilt by their sides. The Trojans had had a grand festival for the victory they thought they had achieved. How wrong were they?

The city was grand with a great marble temple the size of a mountain and as white as freshly fallen snow. This was my first sight inside the giant stone walls of Troy. An impenetrable barrier and we were inside without a fight. A single horse had got us inside, we couldn't lose. Troy was ours for the taking. It would be like taking bread from a servant.

I ordered my men to do their assigned jobs. *Slash! Crash! Bang!* was all I could hear as we slaughtered the so-called untouchables! The Trojans!

James Bedingham (13)
Matthew Arnold School, Oxford

Daedalus And Icarus

I never knew this would turn into a nightmare! My darling son, Icarus, was all happy flying around enjoying his achievement. It was a beautiful sight of him being happy for once. I did tell him not to go too close to the sun. I thought he might have listened or at least heard me for just a bit.

I made another set of wings for myself, so I could be with my son at that marvellous moment! I also told Icarus to stay near the land and not go too far out above the sea. Icarus disobeyed me by flying too close to the sun. This made the wax melt, so the feathers one by one started to fall off. As I watched Icarus plummet it felt like my heart was in my mouth! Icarus dropped like a bird being shot. He just kept falling, falling, falling!

I called his name! No answer! Was he dead? All I could see was a deserted bit of land near where Icarus had fallen. I never saw my darling Icarus again.

Ellie Smith (14)
Matthew Arnold School, Oxford

Daedulas And Icarus

Would it work? Words over and over in my mind. *Would it work?* For years we've been in this tower and now my son goes free. He's there, on the ledge looking around. His emotions are in tangles, he knows not what to do. He must go now. His time has come for freedom. He can walk in the fields and feel more than the cold stone around him. He knows it's time now. He turns his head and looks at me. Large tears rolling down his cheek. He says his final farewells and prepares for his great leap.

My heart misses a beat as he drops off the ledge. I rush towards the window. *He's fallen to his death!* Thoughts run through my mind. As I turn away something catches my eyes and I turn with great haste.

There he is flying away, freedom is now his. Off he goes, his life is now to live. He swoops up high towards the clouds and disappears from my view. He's free at last, he's free. But to my gloom as I stare I see him descend from the clouds. He's not flying with the original grace. He's falling.

As he plummets to Earth again, he will not feel the soft grass of the meadow, but the charred ground of the River Stix. He submerges into the deep, rolling waves. He's dead, he is gone, my beloved son perished. At least no more he suffers. Freedom is now truly his.

Joshua McCaffer (12)
Matthew Arnold School, Oxford

Theseus And The Minotaur

By Venus what have I just let myself into?
   This place stinks, I thought to myself as the impact of the stench came straight at me. As I walked around the beastly labyrinth, unwinding string as I went, I suddenly thought that I may never see my girl again or even the light of day. I began telling myself not to think of all the bad things but all of the good things, so I would be fired up for facing the Minotaur.
   As time went by I kept seeing the skeletons of people who had never even made it to the Minotaur, as they had taken too long to find the middle of the swirling rows of rock.
   'At long last!' I shouted in excitement. I had finally found the middle of the labyrinth but it was quiet, too quiet for my liking. I knew the Minotaur was not too far away.
   At that exact moment in time I heard something behind me. I turned around and there it was, the magical creature itself.
   I drew my sword the creature was puzzled, then it made a sudden attack at me, but I was too quick for that beast.
   After a few minutes I found myself behind it. I chopped off its horn and stabbed its head. It was clearly dead as a squashed bug.

Lewis Knox (11)
Matthew Arnold School, Oxford

Gremlins

Run! The gremlins are here, run for your lives!

They had come from nowhere, they looked so hideous! The smell made me just want to be sick!

As the gremlins approached everyone was running and screaming. As I was running for my life one jumped on my back and had a weird-looking stripe on his head. He bit me! All I remember after that was the excruciating pain.

We worked out that the only thing to kill them was sunlight. We had to trick them into thinking it was dark, so we covered all of the windows while they were destroying everything.

By the time it was light we had to try to uncover the big black sheet. As we yanked it down little dots of light started to shine in and it melted all of the gremlins to the floor. All that was left to do was to clean up all of the mess that they had left behind!

But had they gone?

Sam Matthews (14)
Matthew Arnold School, Oxford

Bermuda Triangle

Wow! My navigation, it's gone wrong, the compass, it's not working. I may need assistance later, for now I'm going to fly straight with the four other pilots. We are flying like a bird with no eyes.

'I'm not sure if you're reading me, hello, hello, *hello!*'

The commander is ignoring my opinions to go west, back home, but he is risking our lives, rampaging on where he wants to go, not realising the fact that he might be wrong about where we are heading. I wish I knew where we were going?

I'm having visions of our Avengers plummeting down one by one like leaves falling off a tree. I'm really nervous, sweating from head to foot with fear as our fuel is going to fail. Soon, frustration is all around me, I'm going to crash and I can't do anything as I just don't know what is happening to my plane. I wish I were somewhere else, I wish I were on land, I wish I were with my family.

This is it, I'm sat here holding a passport-sized photo of my family, next to the lump of iron that is sending me to my grave. The only thing I can do now is wait as I'm running on fumes or pray to my god. There goes Eagle 1, gone into the clouds ... *'Argh!'*

End of transmissions ...

Christopher Benton (14)
Matthew Arnold School, Oxford

Theseus And The Minotaur

I can still remember the darkness of the multitude of terrors in that labyrinth cursed by the gods, that never-ending blackness was my first fear.

I wandered around that maze for an age, and as I walked around through the endless corridors and passageways seeing nothing, I began to doubt everything. I suspected death around every corner, and felt sure that the thread that was my lifeline out of this hellish underworld would snap.

However, as I edged closer to the centre, and the foul stench of rotting flesh entered my nose, I felt real fear of the beast itself. I wondered how many had lost their lives in this graveyard, and I was sure who the next corpse would be.

An hour later I was approaching the centre, which was lit by the soft glow of torches. I paused to sharpen my sword on a stone, although it didn't need it - the blade was of the finest quality. I was delaying and I knew it, putting off the moment when I faced the monster.

When I entered the chamber, I saw the monster immediately. Upright like a man, but with horns, and covered in a shaggy black fur, matted with blood. From the moment I saw it I was gripped by fury that such a thing could exist, and fought with a strength that was not my own.

I stuck my sword in its throat, watched it die with a sense of relief and started retracing my steps.

I didn't look back.

Harvey Frost (12)
Matthew Arnold School, Oxford

The Fall Of Atlantis

It all started the day of the great riot, the people of Atlantis were angry at the gods for a bad season of harvest, of course our gods didn't like this so they punished us, with the fall of Atlantis.

People were screaming, as the waves hit the city walls. Every hit of the waves made huge cracks and crags in the high grey-blue walls. The people knew that the walls were going to collapse and that the seas would come flooding in, we also knew that we had to get out of the city.

Lightning crackled overhead as though the gods were laughing at us, their punishment was fierce, the marshals were shepherding as many of the Atlantians into the tunnels of Neuto as they possibly could. Then the large waves made another crack then another and another. People came screaming and crying towards the caves. Another crack was added and then ... *crack!* I looked up as did many others to see a crack that went from the base of the wall to the top; more importantly, water was leaking through the wall. Then it happened.

First the wall collapsed, then building after building fell. The marshals started to close the rock-faced doors to the caves. I was one of the lucky ones as I just managed to escape, as did about thirty others. I then turned just in time to see the great theatre fall, to see the last glimpse of Atlantis. From then on I realised I would never see the most beautiful city in the world ever again. A city known as Atlantis.

James Little (12)
Matthew Arnold School, Oxford

Theseus And The Minotaur

It's dead. It's finally dead. I've killed the Minotaur.

It all happened yesterday in the dead of night. As I walked into the labyrinth, my heart was pounding like a drum and my eyes were watering. I felt so scared. I turned the corner and, with my head held high, bravely walked down the dark, gloomy passage. A rank smell filled my nose, and it was then that I heard it. A deep, rumbling roar came down the passage to where I stood. As I turned around, I saw it, the Minotaur. It towered above me, waving its huge hairy arms around. I quickly stepped backwards and shrank into the shadows. Fortunately, the beast had not seen me.

As I prepared myself for battle with this huge creature, it suddenly came lumbering around the corner. Its eyes glinted in the flickering firelight from the torch and it began snarling, baring its huge, razor-sharp teeth at me. My mind went blank and sweat poured off of my face. This was it. I was going to die.

In a moment of blind panic, I reached for my sword and began jabbing and slashing at the creature. But it did no good, the more I tried to hurt it, the more enraged the beast became. Its screams filled the cave. I was terrified.

I tightened my grip on the sword and rushed at the Minotaur. As I plunged the sword into its heart, the Minotaur made one last feeble swipe at me, and crashed to the floor, dead.

Bethany Winch (12)
Matthew Arnold School, Oxford

Myths And Legends

He looks amazing like a great human eagle. I watch him step to the edge of the tower window. My heart stops as he takes that lethal step. I can't watch. I close my eyes tightly and grit my teeth.

I open my eyes and to my amazement he is flying, soaring effortlessly in the warm blue sky. I am so proud he is actually doing it, doing it for us so we can have our freedom. I can already hear the crowds and smell the market stalls. I can't wait. Soon he will have reached the coveted land, the promised land.

But wait, he is climbing higher and higher. I know for a fact that the suit I designed for him is made from feathers and wax and cannot survive the sort of temperatures he must be experiencing. To my horror, I can see a small selection of feathers fall from his elegant body, then drips of melted honey and wax as it begins to fall more rapidly, he is losing height.

Finally, after endless screams of terror and struggles to regain control, he plummets to his death. I can hear the splash, the faint efforts to scream, then nothing, only the gentle splashing of the waves breaking on the rocks.

It is as if nothing happened here, as if all is right but it isn't, not by a long chalk. I break down and cry, why have I been so stupid? My final idea of freedom and it has led to my only son's demise.

Georgie Wines (12)
Matthew Arnold School, Oxford

Robin Hood And His Robbery

I knocked on the king's door, my heart pounding like a drum. I couldn't believe I was going to do this. He finally answered and said, 'Hello.'

'Hi, I am a fortune teller, would you like to know what your future holds?'

'OK, sure,' he said.

I entered his carriage, looked around and noticed bags of money and gold. I got out my crystal ball and sat down. I told the king to give me his hand and I pretended to palm read. When I was finished, he pulled his hand away and as he did so I pulled off his rings. The king closed his eyes so I went on to reading the crystal ball. As I was doing that I also grabbed 13 bags of money for my friend to grab as I hung them out the window. The king opened his eyes and said, 'Have you finished yet?'

'Yes I have.'

'OK, you can go.'

I walked out and to the back of the carriage and smiled at my friend. We heard the king shout so we started to run away. Guards started to follow us but we escaped by going through the woods. We got back to a village and as we got our breath back, we went round each house and gave the families that lived there a bag of money each.

I was happy and proud of what I had done.

Bianca Donnelly (12)
Matthew Arnold School, Oxford

King Midas

I throw myself out of my bed, it is cold. I rip my sheets off of my bed and I see gold.

I don't believe it, it's happened, it's true. I pulled the drapes open, 'Argh! What has happened? They've turned into gold. *Oh my God!'*

Everything I touch now turns into gold. I start to touch everything. *'Ha, ha, ha, ha!'* I look rich. I feel as good as gold - that's because everything I touch is gold. When I have friends round I could put the gold in certain places. I would look rich. All I can see is gold, gold, gold!

I run to my wife, with excitement. I find her and tell her what has happened. She looks shocked. I grab her hand and start to pull her, but she makes not one move. I turn around ... my wife, she ... she ... she is gold, *'Noooo!'* What will I do? I feel like my heart has been ripped out of me.

I have to do something, but what? I have to go back to the man who's given me this power. What am I going to do about my wife? I can't just leave her - although I could use her as an ornament in the garden. *No!* She is my wife, well my golden wife.

Oh my God ... I can't eat or drink because it will just turn into gold. My wife has turned to gold. *My life is now over!*

Sophie Gower (14)
Matthew Arnold School, Oxford

Bigfoot

In 1967, my friend Roger Patterson and myself went on a search for the legendary 'Bigfoot'. We travelled by horseback most of the way until ... both of our horses freaked out and got very worried. My horse tried persistently to throw me onto the grimy ground. Roger's horse did throw him off and kicked him in the face! Blood poured out of his head onto the forest floor. I felt like my guts were turning inside my bony body. For a split second I thought he was dead.

As I helped him up he pointed to the horses. They were running away, we had no choice but to let them go. We were in trouble. We had no horses, no food, no Bigfoot and no idea where to go. We stopped and looked around. Nothing. Just trees and mud.

Boom! Bang! Crash! Out of nowhere it came down through the trees like a falling boulder. It got up and came slowly towards us. It must have been nine feet tall at the least. There it was. Big, black, bold and hairy. The so-called Bigfoot. It sounded like a pig, 'Honk, honk, honk.' I pulled out the video camcorder and started to record.

Roger fired a bullet at the monster, but it just bounced off like rubber. It turned and ran like a train through the forest. We had no chance of catching up with it. I was really pleased that we now had evidence of the legendary Bigfoot. We were rich.

I could see the money in my hand but then again would the press believe us? All sorts of bad and nasty thoughts shivered like serpents though my mighty mind. Will our story make us rich or will it be condemned as a hoax?

Craig Skinner (14)
Matthew Arnold School, Oxford

The Mary Celeste

As I read the timid, touching tales of his voyage I cry, I laugh, I smile but ... as I came to the last entry my heart sank and sank and sank deeper and deeper until it could no further, as I read ...

25th November 1872, 8am

It's all over, everything, all of it, over ... It's a windy day, dark and gloomy like a funeral in the village. The Mary Celeste is sailing on course but I fear, that this might be my last entry in my sea log ...

I'm right! The wind is raging, the sea is howling, the boat is dancing a dangerous dance. I can hear my crew yelling, 'Help! Save us, Captain!' but I can't do anything about their fears. I'm glued fast to the floor by my horrors. I can take no more, I just have to close my eyes ...

Oh my lord! Where is everybody? Where am I? Why is it dark? I'm separated from the world like a deer separated from her mother. My heart has been ripped out and fed to the dogs. I have no feelings, no emotions, nothing except questions. Is this the end? What do I do? What's that light ... ? Am I *dead*? *Dead*? *Dead*? ...

And that was the last thing he uttered, but, where is he *now* ... ?

Gemma-Whitney Chobbah (13)
Matthew Arnold School, Oxford

Achilles, The Battle For Troy

That was the day all Trojans would remember! We were approaching the golden beach of Greece. I was thinking to myself, *will I make it?* I was ready to fight for Troy. The waves were pushing us closer and closer to the beach which looked like hundreds of thousands of tiny golden grains.

Bang! We'd landed. Hundreds of Trojans poured out of the ships, like lemmings running off a cliff. The battle had begun! I could hear Trojans and Greeks yelling and screaming 'help' and 'argh'. The blood that was spilt was astonishing. So much blood was shed it could have filled the Pacific Ocean. The beach looked like a sea drenched in blood.

The atmosphere was tense for each side. The heat was boiling hot, blood was flying overhead. The smell was excruciating, of rotting flesh like decomposing bodies in the heat. I knew what I had to do and that was exactly what I was going to do. I was one of the last ones there to celebrate as the victorious living rather than the victorious dead. Today we'd won the battle, but we hadn't won the war.

Sam Byrne (14)
Matthew Arnold School, Oxford

King Midas

10 years ago today was the worst day of my life and still feels as if it was yesterday. If you are wondering what I am talking about I am talking about when I turned my own wife into a piece of gold. You will now ask how did this happen? Well I wanted a spell cast on me that would mean everything I touched would turn into gold. That's right a meaningless piece of gold. What makes it worse is I am a king of all people. From that day on I felt like the world's most selfish and biggest fool.

All I did was raise my hand to give her a hug and show my affection and undying love, and then that was it, right there, when any man's nightmare came true. How would you feel if you turned your partner into a piece of gold which is worth nothing compared to the love you felt for them? Why was I so stupid? So stupid? Now every morning when I awaken I am left with the unforgivable guilt.

As I said I can remember it as if it was yesterday. It smelt as if the palace was filled with the most gorgeous aroma. Everything was so colourful and bright, it was as if there was a rainbow in our palace. Another beautiful and unforgettable smell was the food being cooked. It was the best food you had ever tasted. Unfortunately since my wife died it's as if everything is in black and white. No more tasty food just lumps that make me feel sick. No more gorgeous aromas, but most of all no wife. I have nothing left, just a broken bleeding and bruised heart. What could be worse?

Iona Sinclair (13)
Matthew Arnold School, Oxford

Theseus And The Minotaur

How did I survive in there? Rolling across the floor, being knocked down, not giving me a chance to fight back. But I survived, being scared and nervous thinking, *I'm going to get slaughtered any minute.* But no, I reached for my sword as the bull was about to finish me off. I cut his foot and he fell to the ground.

I managed to get up, even with broken bones. I got my sword, brought it up and stabbed the Minotaur in the heart and killed him. Standing, panting with blood all over me, I left the monster lying there, with my sword in his guts. I fell to my knees and started crying in joy, because I still couldn't believe I was still alive.

I crawled my way out of the maze following the trail I had left. As I got to the entrance, I heard a massive roar of cheers, calling me a hero. I laid there whilst the people still cheered; for now the beast is gone, never to be seen again. Now I'm the local hero.

Conor Merritt (13)
Matthew Arnold School, Oxford

Chapter Of 'Holes'
(In the style of Louis Sachar)

The day Stanley escaped was the hottest yet. Stanley wasn't really bothered by the sun anymore, he was planning. He wasn't sure who he should take with him, or what he should take with him. He was wondering how he should get there, wherever 'there' was. He was thinking about this, when Zero tapped him on the shoulder.

'Want me to dig your hole yet?' asked Zero.

Stanley stared at him for a moment, then clicked out of his trance. 'Yeah, thanks,' he replied. Stanley sat down on the hot, dry earth and went back to his daydream. He thought maybe he might take the warden's car, after all she never used it.

Maybe.

Or he could just go by foot. He was used to walking to the lake every day.

Maybe.

Or he could take the water truck. Zero knew where it was kept at night.

Yes.

Fifteen minutes later the water truck came, with its dust cloud behind it. Mr Sir was driving and Stanley noticed something he had never before. All the mirrors and windows were gone. Had they ever been there? Stanley couldn't remember. He stood there for a minute, wondering.

Then he made his way over to the end of the queue.

Still ... wondering.

Stanley stared at the truck, examining it until it was time for his canteen to be filled. Mr Sir stared at Stanley long and hard as he filled his canteen. 'Thank you Mr Sir,' said Stanley.

When the water truck drove away, Stanley turned around.

The engine was silent.

Charlotte Jeffries (12)
Matthew Arnold School, Oxford

Pandora's Box

I can't believe what I've just done. Why did I do that?

It all started when I was given a beautiful box. I had been told not to open it but I was wondering what was inside. I was so curious that I had to open it so I got the key and slowly opened it up.

The wind howled, the sky turned black. The rain plundered on the roof. It felt like the world had come to an end. A horrible green light glowed from the box. Billions of tiny black things flew out of the window. It seemed to last forever.

When the glow stopped the lid slammed shut. I wiped the tears out of my eyes and approached the box cautiously, I opened it. Nothing happened. I looked inside and there was one of the most beautiful things there ever. Hope.

Thomas Joyce (13)
Matthew Arnold School, Oxford

Myths And Legends

I can't believe what I'm about to do, are the words that keep repeating themselves in my mind as I approach the entrance. My fellow prisoners are wishing me luck but the words sound meaningless as my mind is full of bad thoughts, woes and worries about what I am going to do.

I reach the entrance to the damp, dark labyrinth and go inside.

I can smell the old musky smell of the ancient walls. I can see the rigid and rotting skeletons, scattered all over the floor. My heart is pounding in my chest as I unravel the string I've been given.

After what seems like an age, and I am starting to feel like a mouse scuttling through a maze, I can hear the breathing noise of what sounds like a bull. I turn the corner and there it is, a huge thing with the head of a bull and the body of a man, leering down at me.

I draw my sword, and, with a mighty swing at the thing's neck, slice its head clean off like a hot knife through butter. I slump against the wall, leaning on my sword, and realise that I have done it!

Jack Parry (11)
Matthew Arnold School, Oxford

Theseus And The Minotaur

My God. I cannot believe I am just about to toy with fate and dual the violent murderer of so many innocent lives. I have been wandering through this cursed labyrinth for what seems like days and several annoying times have I crossed over tangled string I have already laid down. I am afraid I am as lost as the town drunk in a hedge maze.

Wait. I can finally hear something. It sounds like an animal panting. I still cannot see anything more than rustic chains and mangled skeletons. It smells of rotten blood and meat with foul dirt and mould thrown in for good measure.

The noise is really loud now and I am really having second thoughts. Perhaps I should turn back. No. I can't. I have come too far. This is it. The fight of the millennium.

I am charging with my sword held high, shouting, 'Death to this evil.' I am swiping at his massive abdomen and feeling confident but he picks me up, not a mark on his furry front. He swings me about like a lifeless rag doll. But I still have my sword, hope is restored. I swing at his arm and it comes straight off. He roars in pain. Then I thrust my sword deep into his bristly thick neck and blood gushes out all over the filthy floor. Then, after a failed cough, my nemesis collapses in the centre of his former arena of terror.

Luke Botham (12)
Matthew Arnold School, Oxford

Daedalus And Icarus

'We've done it!' Daedalus shouted with glee. 'We are finally going to get our freedom, son.'

Icarus stood by the steep edge of the window, with feathered arms which looked like beautiful eagle wings. 'By the gods' father, I can see freedom smiling at us!' Icarus said to his father, looking out at the sun setting. He then stepped out onto the window ledge, the wind blowing at his feathers so vigorously it was pushing him back, as if the wind was stopping him from going. Icarus took a deep breath, so did Daedalus.

Icarus started to flap his feathered arms, then he bravely took a jump. At first, Icarus started to fall slightly, but he flapped his arms harder and faster this time, and then he was up, flying in the air. 'Look, Father, look. I'm finally flying!' he shouted as he started to fly higher.

Icarus was so involved in how he was actually flying, that he forgot about the sun! Of course, Daedalus had worked it out, that if Icarus got too close to the sun, all that honey and wax they had used to stick the feathers on would melt, and the feathers would fall from his feathered arms. But it was no use, Daedalus had tried to call out to his son, but Icarus could not hear him.

Icarus had got higher and higher, then suddenly some feathers started to fall out. Icarus started to fall fast, down and down. Daedalus watched his only chance of freedom and his child fall down and down into the deep blue sea. What had he done?

Eleanor Ewers (12)
Matthew Arnold School, Oxford

An Alternative Chapter To 'Holes'
(In the style of Louis Sachar)

That night Stanley was thinking.
Where is Zero?
Would he come back?
Is he still alive?
Eventually, Stanley realised it was morning.
He pulled on his overalls and edged outside.
The others were in the queue for breakfast.
Already.
Stanley found it strange being at the back of the queue and Zero not being there.
Yet, everything was the same.
Almost.
All day Stanley was threading the same question through his head. *Should he go and find him?*
By the end of the day he had decided.
That night he went around and stole everyone's water canteens and filled them by the parked truck outside.
The guards had fallen asleep.
Luckily.
Stanley made a run for 'God's Thumb'. He knew it was cooler at night.
Usually.
And hotter at day.
Always.
Stanley decided to get as far as he could that night. It was hard as he had to carry seven canteens.
But he knew that he needed them. Stanley's legs grew weak. He could not go much further. Stanley took one more step and collapsed.
Then, he saw him. It was Zero wobbling towards him. Stanley tried to speak but no words came out.
Zero took a canteen and helped Stanley up.
Zero would drink down all of his water.
Usually.
Stanley steadied himself and wiped the sweat off of his head.
It was too hot.

The two of them kept on walking.
Saying nothing.
Not even looking at each other.
As they wobbled into the desert.

Sam Higgs (13)
Matthew Arnold School, Oxford

Perseus And Medusa

I can't believe I'm not just an ornament right now …

I crept, then stopped. Something was coming round the corner, my heart leapt into my mouth. What came round that bend was what I had been fearing. I raised my shield and sword and hoped to live.

The creature was gigantic and had a green tinge to its skin. The body was of human form. The creature had snakes for hair, they were writhing, squirming, all as long as my arm, with fangs as sharp as needles and as long as daggers.

Then it charged, snakes flying, fangs bared. I ended up on the ground dizzy and dazed, with blood in my mouth. I hated the taste of my own blood in my mouth. Now I was getting to know the taste only too well. The creature backed off then lifted its head to the heavens wailing like a banshee. Then as the creature started to lower its gaze towards me, it dawned on me. *How could I have forgotten?* The crab. The gull. The creature before me must not look into my eyes if I wanted to live.

Its gaze reached my shield, it screamed in rage. I ran forwards, swinging my sword in a low arc. It met no resistance. The poisonous blood that ran through its veins now dripped from its headless corpse in an endless stream of drips, scorching the ground where they landed.

Connor Blakey (12)
Matthew Arnold School, Oxford

A Day In The Life Of A Soldier In A Trench

The rain was crashing down like a plane coming in to land and the wind was whistling over the bare treetops of the forest. Gunfire shot down over the moon as soldier after soldier was falling to the ground.

Morning. The sun gleamed like an angel but there was no gunfire since the night raids in Ypres. They got up from the grotty mud of the trench. Screams broke out as soldiers were awoken. Shouts from the commanders said, 'Forward, back, single file.'

Soldiers walked past wounded, ill and dead friends and as they said their goodbyes they knew they had to fight for their country.

The mud turned from brown to red. Paramedics helped the injured but for some brave soldiers it was not enough.

Night fell as fires started to blaze. Soldiers cooked the only rations they could find. They got into their sleeping bags late at night. All fires went out and the soldiers slept dreaming that they were lucky, they were alive!

Joshua Bourton (13)
Matthew Arnold School, Oxford

An Alternative Chapter To 'Holes'
(In the style of Louis Sachar)

'Nice move,' muttered Stanley.

He threw his shovel down and spat in his hole. It wasn't finished, but that didn't matter. He wasn't going to be here much longer.

Stanley stood in the shower. He let the cold water run over his body, then brought the shower down and took a long drink.

He took his canteen and held it under the flow of the water. It didn't take long to fill up.

He didn't know how long it would have to last him, but swiftly he changed into his rest room clothes and walked out onto the lake.

Then he turned as he heard the warden's voice.

'Stanley Yelnats was never here.'

Here!

Here!

It wasn't an echo. It stung in Stanley's mind. It couldn't be an echo. In all this wilderness, there was nothing to echo off.

Nothing!

Nothing!

Something!

Or was it? A fleck of green flashed across the sands.

Stanley ran.

He wasn't quick enough.

Yellow spots glistened like an oasis on a moving body as pain exploded in Stanley's foot. It travelled up his leg, up his arm, until his whole body was engulfed in sweat. The vision of hope faded from Stanley's mind. There was nothing anyone could do to him anymore.

Rose Friedland (13)
Matthew Arnold School, Oxford

An Alternative Chapter To 'Holes'
(In the style of Louis Sachar)

Stanley had decided. The hole he was to dig today would be his last. But how? No one knew, not even himself yet. But maybe, just maybe, it might come to him.

He hoped so anyway.

Stanley tried to find a plan inside his empty head. But one word kept creeping into his mind.

How?

Yet again, for the forty-sixth time he was out in the scorching midday sun, digging what he hoped to be his last hole.

Zigzag had been throwing dirty looks Stanley's way for the past hour or so, but Stanley kept his head down and repeatedly dug his shovel into the dirt, pretending not to care.

He kept an eye out for Zero, but somehow knew that he would not be coming back so soon.

Later that day, as Stanley lugged his sweaty body over to the corner of the shower room, the word 'How' escaped and a plan crept in. A smile broadened across his face. He had it. The way to escape. He thought it over and over again, as he washed his dust-covered body.

The plugs.

That's when he saw it.

The drain.

Quite a big one at that.

Maybe big enough for a Stanley-shaped body.

Then thinking about him and Zero together made him even more eager to get out into the wilderness.

He was to escape.

Tonight.

Melissa Mulvany (13)
Matthew Arnold School, Oxford

Escape From Camp Green Lake
(In the style of Louis Sachar)

Stanley finished his second hole. He spat in it and turned away.

Zero didn't come back.

Stanley lay awake in his crib. He sat up and climbed out.

Was the warden watching him?

He walked out the tent and stepped onto the hot hard muck.

He remembered what he had been told, 'Camp Green Lake had no fences'.

Stanley walked round the back of the shower block and there he saw it.

The water truck.

The door was open and the keys were left in it. Stanley got in. He had never driven a truck before.

'Excuse me,' said the warden as she walked over to the truck.

All of Group D were stood behind the warden.

'Put it into gear!' shouted X-ray.

'Excuse me,' said the warden again.

There was a long stick in-between the two seats. Stanley pulled it back.

He put his foot on the pedal.

Then drove.

Jess Logan (12)
Matthew Arnold School, Oxford

An Alternative Chapter To 'Holes'
(In the style of Louis Sachar)

Yet again, Stanley was in the wrong place, at the wrong time.
 But he wouldn't let it bother him.
 He was leaving.
 For good.
 He wasn't sure when, or how.
 But he was going to be free.
 Soon.
 Stanley woke with a sting on his left butt cheek. His hand shot down to scratch it. Cursing at his itchy hammock he reluctantly got up. He went for a shower and had breakfast. Then he walked drowsily to the shed to get his shovel. He grasped the handle and yelped! There on his palm were two fresh blisters.
 But he wouldn't let it bother him. He was leaving.
 For good.
 Stanley was the first out on the dry dirt. He then saw Zigzag.
 Armpit and Squid trailed out one by one.
 'Hey Caveman! What's up?' cried Squid.
 Stanley raised and lowered one shoulder and began digging in silence.
 Midday came and Stanley began to see the cloud of dust creeping along the wasteland towards them. The truck ground to a halt and Mr Pendanski climbed out to serve the line of red, panting men.
 No one but Stanley noticed the fact that Squid was still sitting quietly in his hole. One after the other the line began to turn and face Squid as he yelled over to Mr Pendanski who strolled over to him.
 Stanley watched from a distance. Turned. Then found himself running toward the front of the water truck, tossing himself through the half open door before turning the rusted keys. He had never driven before. But this time he had no choice.
 After all, he wouldn't let it bother him.
 He was leaving.
 For good.

Hannah Pye (13)
Matthew Arnold School, Oxford

An Alternative Chapter To 'Holes'
(In the style of Louis Sachar)

Stanley woke up from his dream. He had dreamt he was flying.
  Flying out of Camp Green Lake.
  He walked lazily onto the dry, barren wasteland with an empty stomach. He couldn't eat a thing.
  Stanley started digging. Still no one was speaking to him.
  He couldn't even think for himself.
  He dug.
  And dug.
  And dug.
  He looked at his hole; it was barely two feet wide and no more than one foot deep.
  He looked at his empty canteen.
  He looked in all directions in the hope of the water truck, but he soon gave up and turned back to his hole.
  A loud noise gave him a start. It was the supply truck. He thought nothing of it.
  But then something in his brain went 'ping'.
  He sauntered down to the truck. No one liked him anymore, so they didn't look twice at him.
  The supply truck only came once a month, so he wouldn't have many more opportunities.
  He jumped up into the hefty vehicle behind a large crate, then was smashed against the wall as it began to move. He was on his way.
  After what seemed like hours, the truck came to a sudden halt.
  'I'll just go and take the crate inside the shop, OK?' said one of the drivers.
  'Sounds fine by me!' said the other.
  'You wait 'ere.'
  Stanley hadn't thought about other supplies.
  The men removed the crate ...
  ... He couldn't get out of this one ...

Josie Pye (13)
Matthew Arnold School, Oxford

Odysseus And The Cyclops

'My god, we have to get off this island.'

Just after the men thought they were home free, the Cyclops, still blinded by the sharpened tree trunk in his one eye, was on their trail. He was following the scent of the fine wine they had brought him to seduce him into going to sleep.

'Run! Run!' said Odysseus. 'Let's ditch the sheep and get to the boat before he gets any closer.'

Just as they left the sheep that had helped them get out of the Cyclops' cave, the Cyclops tripped on a boulder, but he didn't get up - he paused for a second.

'Why has he stopped? What is he thinking? What are we waiting for …? Let's get a move on…'

As the men ran, the Cyclops got closer, but when they got to the boat the Cyclops had fallen again, so the men had time to cast off and set sail in victory.

Michael Njuguna (13)
Matthew Arnold School, Oxford

Theseus And The Minotaur

I can still feel my heart throbbing now. But it was such a thrill, yet relieving for my friends and I.

When I saw his fiery red eyes, I was determined to defeat this creature, half man, half bull

I found my way searching round the winding maze, laying down the golden thread behind me to find my way back. I reached the middle.

There it was. Feeding on one of the innocent villagers to keep it happy. I was ready to do this deed. I drew my sword up, held it in both hands, ready to plunge it deep into his insides.

He dodged out the way, knocking the sword out of my hands and sliding across the floor, hitting against the solid stone walls. He flung himself towards me, shoving me to the floor and leaping upon me.

He looked into my eyes with his drool splashing across my face. I slowly reached down to my sock and slyly slithered out my dagger. I clenched it in my palm and stuck it into his heart. He stopped then rolled off me, lying on the dusty damp floor. I got to my feet and picked up my silver shiny sword. I took a big swing and sliced off his head.

Josh Kenyon (13)
Matthew Arnold School, Oxford

Escape From Camp Green Lake
(In the style of Louis Sachar)

The night Stanley Yelnats escaped was hot. He was waiting, waiting for something to happen. Anything.

He was waiting until everything was perfect - tonight was that night. It was hot with a little cloud in the sky.

Stanley crept out of Tent D.

He made a break for the cupboard where the shovels were kept.

He had to dodge the holes. He thought it was like a game he used to play.

Unfortunately for Stanley it was locked, so he had to get the key from the warden's cabin.

First he tried the door.

It was open.

He crept past the warden.

She was sleeping.

He went to the bathroom where he saw the pink flowered make-up case. He tried to forget what had happened the last time he was here.

He was looking for the key. There was a hook above the flowered case.

There it was.

He crept back out.

He went back across the lake, but halfway across he spotted Mr Sir. Luckily it was where a group of holes were, so he checked one and it was clear. He jumped into it.

It took ten minutes before Mr Sir left, so he ran to the cupboard and luckily, the second key he tried worked.

He took the shovel.

He ran out of camp to try to find Zero. He had taken the shovel because he had thought it might come in handy.

He was right!

Jenny Briggs (12)
Matthew Arnold School, Oxford

Daedalus And Icarus

'Quick, they're coming! Jump!'

Why have I just encouraged my precious only son to leap off this isolated cliff-top tower? Will he fly? My heart is pounding so fast, I feel like it's going to escape from my chest. I pray Icarus remembers all my instructions to keep to the middle altitude. High enough to avoid the azure ocean with its dangerous spray, low enough so that the heat of the sun will not melt the beeswax that holds the feathers together.

Oh where is he? I hear screeching eagles circling effortlessly overhead, but where is Icarus? As I scour the horizon, with utter relief, out of the white-hot sun, I see my beloved boy gliding high into the cloudless sky. The terror on his face gradually being replaced by an overwhelming smile. I scream to him, 'You're free, we've done it!'

Minutes later, helplessly, I witness with horror Icarus drunk from the thrill of flying, soaring too near to the sun. My desperate pleas to reduce height are blown back in my face by the breeze. I can only hope.

In disbelief I see wax and feathers disintegrating from the wings. Then suddenly Icarus plummets to the sparkly Aegean Sea with a splash. What's left of the wings floats to the surface but there's no sign of my son. Panic overcomes me as I rush down the cliff side. Full of guilt, I look out to the unforgiving sea.

Sarah Foster (12)
Matthew Arnold School, Oxford

Alternative Chapter To 'Holes'
(In the style of Louis Sachar)

The escape day was hot.

Too hot.

Stanley woke up and, as usual, he went out to dig his hole. On the horizon, Stanley saw the cloud of dust as the water truck came nearer.

He knew this was the time.

Stanley queued with the other boys to get his canteen filled. He thanked Mr Pendanski and returned to the hole. As the truck pulled away, he went. He stared over at the tents.

'Hey! Caveman, where are you goin'?' shouted Zigzag.

Stanley ignored them.

'I'll bet he's goin' to teach Zero to read!' replied X-ray.

Stanley walked on.

He knew where he wanted to go, but he couldn't do it alone.

As he reached the tents, he heard an angry voice.

'A ... B ... C ...'

'Zero!'

Stanley stumbled into the tent.

'Hey Zero, how do ya want to get out of here?'

Zero said nothing.

'Zero, how do ya want to get out of here?'

Zero said nothing.

Stanley turned to go.

'Wait!'

Zero stood up to follow.

Outside the tent, the two boys stood side by side.

Stanley stared longingly at the big thumb.

They heard a familiar voice behind them.

'Excuse me.'

The warden looked down at her nails.

'Hmm, could do with some more nail polish I think.'

Stanley shuddered.

Jess Beasley (13)
Matthew Arnold School, Oxford

Escape From Camp Green Lake
(In the style of Louis Sachar)

The day Stanley escaped was the hottest yet.
He and Zero started digging their trench at six in the morning and finished at six at night. Stanley had completely forgotten about teaching Zero how to read and write. All they wanted to do was to be free and happy. One of the main problems was the heat. It was the hottest day yet. They had finished for the day and they had had their showers and felt great.

But when they were on their way to the wreck room they heard, 'Zero, Stanley, get here now!' screamed Mr Pedanski. 'I won't say a word if you let me in your little tunnel escape.'

'Excuse me,' whispered the warden.

Mr Pendanski had just landed himself in very deep water.

The next morning when the warden went to wake the brutes up, Zero and Stanley were gone. The warden was just starting to believe Mr Pendanski about the escape. So what will or can she do?

To the disbelief of the warden at dinner that night, she found Mr Pendanski with blisters on his hands from digging. The warden was absolutely furious. She was in the mood to kill. She looked out the window and she could see Zero and Stanley on their way to freedom.

Adam Felix (13)
Matthew Arnold School, Oxford

Theseus And The Minotaur

What have I done to deserve this? Why did I agree? All of those people are being eaten alive! I'm walking down a corridor, the dirty, filthy, bloodstained gravel crunching under my feet. The walls are covered in slime and blood. I turn the corner and there lay a headless skeleton, clothes torn and ripped cover its body and a foul stench rising.

What was that? I spin around and see nothing but a shadow race round the corner. I carry on down another path, alert and tense, sweat running down my face and sword. Again I hear movement behind me and spin around to see a great bulk in the shadows, its huge red eyes staring at me, the great bloodstained horns pointing towards me. I dive for my life. The horn's sharp point narrowly missing my torso. I manage to slice open the beast's belly causing it to roar in pain and anger. The monster stopped at the far end of the path and swung around to face me once again. Again it charged at me, but this time I was ready. I dived to the right and flicked my sword up towards its face, tearing an eye out. The beast was vulnerable!

I charged, sword out in front, stabbing it in the face and belly many times. Finally I beheaded the foul beast. The body fell to the ground, blood pouring out of the wounds. Finally, the beast is dead! No more innocent lives need be wasted. Where is the string?

Daniel Pickard (13)
Matthew Arnold School, Oxford

Escape From Camp Green Lake - Chapter from 'Holes'
(In the style of Louis Sachar)

The night Stanley escaped was the coldest yet. He and Zero were plotting to escape from Camp Green Lake. They had been plotting for six weeks now, but they needed to do it without anyone noticing.

They talked about it for a long time when Stanley taught Zero to read. But when X-ray turned up and said, 'Well, well, well, escaping from Green Lake eh?'

Stanley walked towards him and X-ray shouted, 'Wonder if the warden knows?'

Stanley tried to stop him from shouting it out loud.

He gave in and said, 'We're leaving tomorrow morning, if you really want to come.'

'Alright then,' replied X-ray.

Zero was behind them writing as neat as possibly.

X-ray walked out singing, he said, 'Tender Stanley.'

They woke up twenty minutes before the horn went. They got their breakfast before the water truck came to fill their canteens.

When Mr Sir went to see what Zigzag had found, X-ray stole the water truck and started the engine. The three convicts drove to the nearest town in Texas and sold the water truck. They went home and were both followed.

So just wait till Derrick Dunne meets X-ray!

X-ray whispered to Stanley, 'Tender Stanley.'

Ryan Smith (12)
Matthew Arnold School, Oxford

Escape From Camp Green Lake
(In the style of Louis Sachar)

Everyone was asleep.
> He hoped.
> He was in his tunnel and on his way to freedom.
> He hoped.
> He was thirsty, he knew.

This had all started when Stanley was thinking about Zero, how he escaped and if he were still alive. He couldn't stop thinking about him. He knew that no one had expected Zero's break-out, but now, everyone knew that there was going to be a break-out. It's just when. If he was going to escape, he would have to do it silently.

Every night, after digging a hole, he came back to camp and dug a bit of his tunnel. He borrowed a piece of wood from the wreck room to cover the entrance to the tunnel. He put a bit of mud over it to make it look normal. Soon his tunnel was nearly 50ft long. If his spade were 5 foot long, that is.

At last he was out. Daylight. He was free.

He could just see Camp Green Lake. He could also see Mr Sir coming straight towards him in the water truck.

So he ran.

And ran.

And ran, until he could run no more, until he could not see or hear Mr Sir.

Ryan Louise (13)
Matthew Arnold School, Oxford

The Return Of Frankenstein

I waited for what seemed like hours as the thing I had created groaned and squirmed in the leather straps wrapped around it. I felt a bead of sweat run down my cheek. I heard something snap. Suddenly it was quiet and I heard a shout outside. Forcing myself to look out I saw a mob. Each holding a torch in their hand and some form of defence in the other. They were smashing at the door. It was over. I closed my eyes and prayed. A deep groan echoed down the hall to me and I knew it was coming. My mouth was dry, my head spinning.

A lumbering figure emerged at my door. I looked at my creation, the monster I had created. No! It was much more than that, much more than a monster, it was hideous, miserable and deformed. I looked again at the beast I had created and I saw my dead mother, grave worms in her flannel and I fainted! The last thing I saw was the monster picking me up off the ground and I felt Death's warm embrace. I knew that if I wasn't killed by the monster, the mob would certainly do it instead.

Shan Ahluwalia (13)
St Martin's School, Northwood

Letter From The Front Army Camp
(Response to 'The Charge of the Light Brigade' by Alfred Lord Tennyson)

Balaclava 1485

My esteemed parents,

I write to you in this triumphant hour. The night is bitterly cold. I write with the glint of my sabre in the half darkness. I am still glad that I joined the army. You must not worry about me. Those evil Cossacks and Russians have captured our guns. Lord Lucan is said to have asked Captain Nolan to recapture the guns. That is all we brave soldiers can talk about.

I have a beautiful dappled-grey horse named William. At night when all warmth deserts me and I lie on the green-jewelled and dewed grass, I snuggle up next to him and he warms me up as if I were in a blazing furnace. William is the only real friend I can rely on, that is apart from Charles, who camps next to me.

His mother is living in the same part of London as you. She owns a shop too. It is a blacksmith shop called 'Metal Wonders'. It is quite close to our shop, so if you see it, pop in and say hello to her.

Charles is about my size with red hair, as if it were a raging fire. He has a great sense of humour and writes some witty poetry.

You will be pleased to know that I have kept my uniform clean. I was given a delicate cherry plume, which gently brushes the side of my neck in the cold breeze. We have stationed ourselves in a position straight in front of a never-ending valley in the mist. All the pessimistic men called it the 'Valley of Death', but it is surely not dangerous.

From your humble son, Peter.

Rohan Dey (12)
St Martin's School, Northwood

The Woman In Black Review

'The Woman in Black' is one of the best plays I've seen in a very long time. As I began to take my seat I realised I was about to see a great play, just by looking at the stage and the posters that surrounded me. As it began the stage went dark and a man walked in. For about the first ten minutes I began to fall asleep, but then it became interesting. From the moment the 'Woman in Black' walked in, I knew it was going to be a production I wasn't going to forget.

I thought it was really good how there was a limit to the props they used, for example, for a large picnic basket it was used as a horse cart, a bed and a cabinet for documents which I thought was really clever.

The way they used the lighting was incredibly clever because of the see-through curtain and you could really imagine what was actually there. The actors were very good. I liked the suspense because it kept me wondering where the 'woman in black' actually was.

My opinion was that this play was amazing. I hadn't seen a play in a very long time, but this made me want to see this play over and over again.

Jonathan Barker (13)
St Martin's School, Northwood

A Day In The Life Of A Boy On The Titanic

The rain slashed down as the cold Atlantic wind whipped in my face. The ship had just been wrecked by, as rumour had it, an iceberg. There was a frantic rush of flowing people, desperately searching for their loved ones. But I stood patiently with my mother in the long queue for the boat, waiting and hoping.

'It'll be okay,' my mother whispered to me reassuringly, but I could hear the uncertainty in her voice. I shivered. The pitch-black sky above me, seasoned with glistening and gleaming stars, almost mocking my position.

'I'm sorry,' the sea captain said. 'No more space.' But then he turned to face me, 'Actually,' he began, 'you might just be able to fit on as you are small. But no one else or the boat will overturn.'

I turned towards my mother, trying to tell her to let me stay with her, but I was already being hauled onto the boat. I lay cramped, worried and scared, desperately wanting to go back to my mother, but the boat was already going. I looked around at the strange people who were accompanying me. They all looked tense, frightened and worried.

As the boat sailed away into the velvety-black emptiness, I turned round to have a last look at the face of my mother as the Titanic plummeted down into the deathly cold waters of the Atlantic.

Shabbir Merali (13)
St Martin's School, Northwood

The Condemned Prisoner

I was sitting, tired and lonely, in a prison cell in Newgate Prison. The floor was damp and filthy with a sewer running through. The squalid smell of the sewer smelt worse than the inside of a toilet. The walls had fungus growing on them and looked like mini forests. The ceilings were as high as a house and as dirty as a car that had not been washed for two years. Green algae dripped off the ceiling like sticky, sloppy slime.

Muffles of sound came through the thick, dark, black bricked walls. The trace of sound sounded like speaking to someone who has their hands in their ears to the listener. Minute strands of light peeped through the old grilled windows, forming patterns on the black floor. The grimy window was as small as an A4 sheet of paper.

I was wearing torn, dusty rags covered with dirt. I was half naked and smelt of rotten eggs because I had not had a shower for over a month. Scuttling rats and cockroaches clambered through the grimy cells.

Suddenly, a sound. Someone was coming. Light filled the cell like water filling a glass. I had to cover my eyes due to the bright light which filled the room.

'Some men shall come to take you to Tyburn tomorrow. There, you will be hung. Understand?' barked the guard in a casual tone. He sounded as if he did not care that I was going to die. He probably did not. Then he left. That was all. Again, the cell was dark and gloomy.

Mohsin Saleh (12)
St Martin's School, Northwood

Soldier

He fell down, sprawling in the mud. He coughed up blood. He lay spluttering, trying to regain his breath. He could hear his heartbeat and felt the blood pulse through him. The pain rushed down his arm. He let out a screech of agony as he felt the hot lead settle further into his skin. It was unheard over the noise of others falling to the clatter of the guns.

The blood slowly trickled out onto the thick mud. He had had no sleep that night. No one had. The Germans had not stopped attacking as they knew the English were wearily retreating. Summing up all the strength he could muster, he hauled himself into the think hole the trench that was his station. The helmet and heavy leaded boots almost sent him back down sprawling in the mud.

Soft, sweet memories of Eliza filtered into his mind. He was protected from the harsh, cruel world around him. This happiness was over in but a moment as another man fell down with a ghoulish scream of pure pain. Then nothing. He lay with the others that lay strewn on the boggy marsh, tossed like a spoilt child's unwanted toys, by numerous gas attacks and nailing shells. He put the heavy rifle back on his shoulder. He looked above. The clouds in the sky were cracked like fragmented bits of stone scattered across the sky.

The sun seemed a deep crimson in the early hours of the morning.

Alex Freethy (13)
St Martin's School, Northwood

Child Memory

I reluctantly packed my dog's belongings in a cardboard box. His favourite toy was a tug-of-war rope. Then I packed his green lead at the top. We were waiting at our house for the middle-aged couple to pick Smudgie up. I was seven years old and I was very sad when I was told that my dog, who I really enjoyed playing with and loved, was leaving. I nearly started crying. Then the people came to pick Smudgie up. I felt as if I wanted to stop them from taking my dog away, but I knew that I couldn't. They strapped him up and we said our goodbyes to him. They waved at us and they drove off.

There was water gathering up in my eyes. I couldn't hold it for very long and then I burst out crying. I remembered how comfortable it felt when I cuddled him and played with him. I felt as if he had been gone a long time and I couldn't bear it without him being there. Then I had a flashback of when it was my birthday. He was jumping and barking. He gave me a look with his eyes fixed on me and his mouth opening slowly to tell me to play with him or he would start barking. I picked up the ball and he jumped on me as if he was trying to push me over. Then I thought we should go to the park. I unclipped the lead and he went about sniffing. His nose was a cauldron colour with two holes at the bottom. His fur was a sunburnt colour with patches of orange on his body. Then the flashback ended.

Nikhil Patel (11)
St Martin's School, Northwood

Letter From The Front

Army Hospital, Scutari - 27th October 1854
My beloved parents,
The brigade has endured much tragedy. Betrayed by orders, we charged down a godforsaken valley, harassed by cannon fire.

As we galloped, there were deafening noises and we were rained on with shot and shell; but still our tide of cavalry continued to swarm forward, charging through the enveloping pall of smoke. The gallant blue and red doublets charged into the mist, engulfed by veils of acrid smoke which hid the churned mud and pools of dark blood. There was constant noise from the cracks and booms of the Russian guns, mixed with screams from men and horses.

I saw Cossacks and Russians reeling from my swinging sabre strokes as I surged forward. Then the guns silenced and the smoke rose, I saw the full horror around me.

As I peered through the rising clouds, I saw my friend, trapped under his lifeless horse. I helped him to move the poor animal and we both climbed onto my strong steed, to escape from this scene of death and devastation.

We cantered down the valley, dodging the lifeless corpses and wounded men, constantly harassed by the Russian gunfire and trying to dodge the cannonballs, which flew through the air around us - but I was hit and fell.

My dearest parents, I am safe and in the hospital at Scutari. Many died for no reason. I was lucky to escape. May God protect us all.

Your loving son,
Charles Constable.

Charles Constable (11)
St Martin's School, Northwood

Extract From The Haunted School

The old, rotten, wooden front door of the school was jammed, with only a small gap that we could climb through. Once inside the hallway of the school, it was all smothered in a black charcoal substance from the fire. The moonlight shone through the cracks in the blinds which, torn from sharp debris, had obviously fallen in from the roof. This made the room wet and damp.

The chandelier hung desperately away from the ceiling, making it look as if it were gasping for fresh air. The computer from the secretary was on its last wire, stopping it from falling off the rotten, wooden table.

'Argh,' screamed Sam seeing a dirty, fat rat lying helplessly dead in front of the staircase.

The three boys ran as far as they could away from the rat, up the grand staircase.

'Woo, that was a close one,' said Kushal gasping for breath.

'Shh,' said Sam, 'can you hear that banging coming from the loft?'

Samuel Klein (13)
St Martin's School, Northwood

River Walk

It was an amazingly stormy day. Strong winds and vicious rain stopped me from going forward. A lot of raindrops blocked my sight. I squinted through the rain and suddenly I could see an old, rusty, metallic bridge, slightly.

Rusty Coke cans were being blown across the surface of the violent water. I regarded the turbulent river. A rotting boat bobbed crazily like a small, drowning child in a deep swimming pool, and also I saw the fractured, tangled brown branches of twisted trees.

I peered into the foggy depths. It was like mad, ochre sandstorm in the desert. Many boulders, rocks and small stones swirled in the wild water.

Abruptly, the bright sunshine merged through the gaps of the gloomy storm clouds.

Yuki Yoshimura (12)
St Martin's School, Northwood

Walk About

Walking can be exciting, but also dangerous.

The noble trees, brown, tall, old, a bit like my grandfather, stood soldier-like. At night they show a dark side, so powerful that all is forgotten after they finish. Their first tactic is to crowd around once the forest is entered. Then they secretly and purposely attempt to brush their long, crooked, wrinkled bristles against the shoulder to scare.

Their third intention is to trip, using their hooked roots, and once on the ground, always on the ground.

Bushes talk, trees torment. Devious animals get up to no good.

In the other environment ... the smooth, soft, gentle breeze leaves me breathless, like a beggar who hasn't seen food for three weeks. The Sunday stroll is awakening. Passing trees which wobble in the breeze like jelly. The lovely birds chirp and the winds whistle to create a beautiful orchestra. The rustling of the leaves joins in along with the scraping of the trees to produce a symphony.

The church stands high, confident and smart. When entered, the power of awe takes place. When walked out of, the feel of guilt and bad conscience is vanished.

The beautiful river blows the worries away and relaxes like a cross between a pill and a bomb settling the mind in your own world. The pain, all gone as if a cheetah has captured and feasted on its prey. The fragile waves break instantly when they touch the boundaries. The elastic bends are withstanding the pain of stretching.

Azaan Mohamed (11)
St Martin's School, Northwood

Dingy Street

One spooky autumn's night I was walking alone on a dingy street. It was so quiet I could hear a rat scurrying along the cold stone ground. It was so dark I could hardly see anything, until I saw a candle flickering, which made a terrifying shadow. It looked like a drunk person coming towards me, but it was very strange because I could not hear any footsteps. After that it fell silent again, until the silence was shattered by more footsteps; not just mine, but someone else's. I stopped and so did they. I walked again and so did they and then, out of the pitch-black darkness came a man who was looking for money to buy a drink from further down the street. I ignored him and carried on walking.

As I continued on down the road, it started to stink from decaying waste and rubbish. The smell made me feel sick. Suddenly, I heard something running towards me. My heart was pounding. I was very frightened, but it was only a cat in the tight alleyway. *That was lucky,* I thought. Just then, up ahead I saw something that gave me hope. I started running towards it, but then I could feel the path was getting narrower and narrower. It felt like the walls were closing in on me. I made a quick decision to go and get out of there.

Finally I made it to the end. I could now smell the sodden barrels of ale. It was so disgusting, but I soon forgot about it when I saw the light ahead again. As I went towards it, the glowing light started to get closer and closer. Eventually I reached it, but it was only a lamp from the pub. I could hear the rusty metal gate creak at its hinges, and the wooden sign swaying in the wind, which was getting stronger by the minute. I could feel things being whipped up onto my face. It hurt because dust got into my weary eyes.

Hasaan Ausat (12)
St Martin's School, Northwood

The Journey Around My Kitchen

Even if I were blindfold, I could find my way to the kitchen, because the smells from Mum's cooking are so strong. But the first thing I notice when I enter the room is the fish bowl and the light behind it, which makes my fish glow a beautiful golden colour. My attention is immediately distracted by the sound of the potatoes bubbling up, which remind me of natural springs, where the bubbles rise to the surface.

When my mum asks me to fetch some meat from the freezer, I reach my hand into the freezer grabbing hold of what seems like an iceberg, or a rather small rock, but it is actually the meat that Mum has asked for.

Next to the freezer there is a window, which not only gives us a fantastic view of the garden, but also acts as a window on the weather.

On the other side of the kitchen I can see a bowl which has the remains of chocolate icing, but is about to be washed up in the sink. I lunge at the bowl before Mum cleans it and I wipe my finger in my mouth. It tastes like paradise.

George Clark (12)
St Martin's School, Northwood

Isolation

The long, swerving river like a great python that coils and entangles the molten, red cliff. The sun is invisible, but still reflects on the huge, dusty brown cliffs.

The wall of cliffs is stalking, anticipating action, like a rattlesnake in a dry, arid prairie, violating its prey to let its focus down for one second to strike.

The bushes are like a styled hedgehog. The sand just shimmers lowly in comparison. The clouds are a timid white rabbit, slowly surveying its surrounding from the sanity of its own little hovel.

The parched land is cracked like a complex jigsaw. The cliffs red, like a setting sun floating on the horizon, as if on a boat drifting out of human eyes.

Alex Cockerham (11)
St Martin's School, Northwood

In The Eyes Of ... A D-Day Landing Troop

The landing boat hit the sand, the door swooped open and the soldiers flooded out. A barrage of bullets flew towards my platoon, taking out over half of my comrades. I struggled through the water and ran for cover under a rusty metal barricade. Bullets glided over my head, making a sizzling noise. Men were dropping to the ground like dead fish in a barrel.

I grasped my rifle in my hands and took sight at a German soldier perched in the pill box. My finger tightened on the trigger and the bullet seared out from the gun. I felt disgraced to take the life of another man, but I knew they would do the same to me. I placed my face on the bloodstained beach, taking cover, scared for my life.

My comrades called me, telling me to move forwards but I couldn't, I was stuck to the ground fearing for my life. What would it be like if I were to die? My wife and child, what would they do? Where would they go? I knew I had to survive for them. I picked myself up from off the ground and ran forwards, ducking and diving, weaving in and out of my dead friends.

My platoon had all been murdered, the other soldiers dead, only a couple of hundred soldiers remained on the beach with me. I could not tell what laid before me, all I knew is that I had to live.

Elliott Edwards (13)
St Martin's School, Northwood

Cuba Morning

The blood-red sun ascends over the grey-lined horizon into the opalescent sky. The blackness of the sleepy night slowly dies away, fading into the air ...

The first of thousands of gulls sweeps over the placid sea, squawking as the deep blue water shimmers as coins of light shine on them. The night had been violent, the waves had crashed against the cliffs and torn away at the shore, tearing away, and all was now calm. The sea whispered secrets to the sky while it gently washed onto the shore and then fell back. It was deep blue, the blue when one has just exploded with rage.

The waves shivered and rattled as they bore against the land and the dark glow of the sun blackened the palm trees that fringed the coast and the beach. Fishing boats bobbed on the water, tired and nodding off to sleep as the lustre light of the sun gently glowed onto the sails, etching dancing shadows over the constantly rising and falling water. As fish foolishly got trapped in the nets, the fishermen dozed in their hammocks with straw hats drawn over their faces, and their mouths gnawing at fresh rolls of tobacco, eyelids gently falling as they fell once again to sleep.

The sea washed away the sun's blood from its open wound as morning approached Cuba, and soon the beach's ghostly silence would die away into the air as tourists would come to the beach that morning, that Cuba morning.

Nikhil Patel (13)
St Martin's School, Northwood

Prologue

Rain tore down, battering on the pirates' small, splintered rowing boat. Clouds loomed just above their heads, creating an eerie mist around them. Darkness lingered. Silence. The boat steered, slicing through the mist. The paddles were deep in the purple water.

A man stood at the bow of the boat, scratching his infected ear. He had cruel eyes, sharp, rotting, yellow teeth pointed down from his mouth like stalactites in a cave. His face was ugly; he had a square chin and a scar down his left cheek. His body was unbelievably large and in complete disproportion to his head. Every centimetre was crammed with bulging muscle. His skin was dirty and his hair was like long black straw.

The men that sat at the bottom of the boat were his men, and the men knew him as Barbarosa. He was second in command of 'The Cobra'. They were the most ruthless and dangerous gang of pirates in the world.

The boat slithered along the water through the thickening mist. It was getting darker; huge pine trees towered above, staring at them. The water was slashing, jumping from the depth of the ocean and tearing silently at their faces. Suddenly it appeared. Looming from the shadows, a skull, and a horrific X-ray of what is behind the flesh of a human's head, it stood fifty feet tall, snarling at them, warning them to come no further, but Barbarosa knew that no one would come to look for it here.

Greg Zimmerman (12)
St Martin's School, Northwood

Mystic Oceans

A storm was brewing. The ocean swayed to and fro, heavy rain beat down, and the ship rocked to the beat. The waves grew higher and higher and crashed down upon us, mocking our size as they fell. I clung to the side of the ship as the daunting wave came upon me. The wave pounced upon the boat and knocked me and part of the ship off. I was floating on a piece of rotting wood which came from the boat. The water was cold, so cold that it was painful. It was like the grip of death. I gasped with anguish and shock as salty water filled my lungs. The taste of salt was strong in my mouth, and I was strangled by the acrid stuff in my throat and lungs.

But it was the cold that was most distressing. I felt that I could survive until after a few minutes great waves crashed down upon me. As the waves came down, I struggled to hold onto my float. My float was knocked away and I floundered in the water, struggling to stay afloat. Half-drowned, I resurfaced, gasping for clean air and this nightmare to end. I thought I saw ghostly wraiths crashing down amongst the waves. The shroud was hot against my neck. The skies were black with death, as they mockingly watched my struggle.

There was one victor here, but that would have to be revealed to me later.

Richard Gallagher (12)
St Martin's School, Northwood

The Hazy Coastline

There were white hotels and sloping rooftops that blurred in the hazy distance as the sweep of the bay became engulfed in mist and drizzle. The cool azure glistened in the sunlight. A tranquil air out of sinister beauty hung in the ultramarine bay, whilst ghostly white mountains loomed in the distance.

The mountains were like sleeping giants, guarding the city, keeping the outsiders at bay. The dark, smoky clouds swayed to and fro, looking like nibbled pieces of candyfloss as the golden-crusted sun was forced to fall.

The onyx leaves surrounded the vivid, sedate scenery; the immense, extensive mountains caught my eye, sitting on their majestic thrones. A tractor vivaciously rolled along the coral and opal grass. The Pacific stream was inspected in absolute tranquillity, by the ravishing ultra sun. One or two cotton clouds reflected off the aqua metallic river.

The pea-green forest in the distance felt as if there was a football match going on. The branches looked like they were going to grab you. The trees felt happy when I gazed at their bare, bony bodies. I felt like there was a huddle and a meeting going on between themselves.

The houses were situated in an unusual spot with no scenery near the lonely cottages. There were all kinds of birds chirping everywhere you looked.

The river, glistening in the sun's rays, was full of exuberant life as it was mainly fast-flowing throughout, but there was one amazing part with lots of beauty and that was just before the glistening blue water like an Hawaiian sea.

Hamza Sheikh (12)
St Martin's School, Northwood

My Grandmother

She stands, tall and firm, always in command. Her hair is a luscious black, streaked with snow-white cotton hair. The sun's beams enhance her light brown face, which is covered in walnut-like wrinkles. Her ears are sprayed with colours of gold and a sparkling white; the untouched earrings lay in their sockets for sixty-four years.

Her lips are moulded of a pink and dark red. Her silk saree is wrapped all the way round her body. The slow, tortoise-like strides only carry her ten metres in length. Her voice as quiet as a mouse, shoots out words so strong and powerful, it sounds like a war. Her wooden cane is painted a vibrant black.

Her handbag is encrusted with the finest leather that forms the frame and the best needlework of roses, lilies and daisies forms the middle. Her brown leather sandals are strapped tightly to her feet. Her smooth coat is worn like a straitjacket to stop the cold penetrating her skin. Her cackle of a laugh is heard by everyone in the room. I love my grandmother.

Sajan Shah (13)
St Martin's School, Northwood

Boiling Bubbles - A Kitchen Scene

I dawdled into the steamy kitchen. A cooking smell instantly reached my nose and my mouth started watering. Mum flung the double doors open and sunlight streamed through, splattering the floor tiles like an abstract artist.

Boiling bubbles gathered for a meeting in the throbbing heart of the saucepan. The hob caught alight and made a small whoosh, like a mouse blowing on a fire. A shiny red pot sat on the hob, his next-door neighbour foaming fiercely. Straggling strands of spaghetti slipped into the saucepan flailing their weedy arms behind them. The sharp knife cracked on the chopping board after slicing mercilessly through a helpless onion. A cool breeze drifted into the room like a silent ghost, sifting through my hair as if checking for something. The bin clanged noisily, like cymbals clashing together at the climax of a Christmas hymn.

The dog clambered in, slipping on the wet tiles and colliding with the gnawed cupboards. Wafts of smoke rose from the spaghetti-filled saucepan, curling and twisting in the air. Chicken cracked and spat delightfully on the grill, as an orchestra of smells permeated the room. Boiling bubbles in the pan.

William Pithers (11)
St Martin's School, Northwood

Countryside Scene

I sat on the beautiful, fresh, warm, clean grass, the willows beside me filtered the sunlight and made warm beams of light heat my frozen body. I looked out at the totally undisturbed countryside. It was amazing to see such a calm, smooth lake. The water was glistening with a sheet of gold as the soft light reflected off the water's surface. I looked up to see totally snow-covered mountains in the distance, with a ring of white, fluffy, elastic clouds. There was also an astonishing azure blue sky. It was so quiet that you could hear a rock falling or a twig snapping from miles away. On the other side of the lake, lay a herd of grazing deer, while rabbits were playfully chasing each other in the thick, forest-like grass.

As it was spring, many beautiful flowers like daisies and daffodils filled the area. I walked round the lake while the wind brushed against my hair. Lots of blossom fell and flew in the wind. When I reached the other side of the lake, the deer and rabbits continued their day. I sat down again, only to hear and see many birds with amazing voices and colours, that flooded the sky with excitement. I remembered coming here when I was a child with my friends, always trying to catch rabbits but we never made it. The hours were passing and I had to go home, back to my worried parents. I took a picture of the sunset over the golden lake with pink, candyfloss-like clouds, and left ...

Christian Shephard (12)
St Martin's School, Northwood

Mist

The white blanket of mist hung over the tall, dead building of trees. The field of water vapour blocked the ever-growing brightness of the sun. The solitary silent mist suffocating the ground covered with ferns. The oxygen released by the trees and ferns consumed by the darkening mist, drained of its life.

The field of mist enclosed from every direction. Ferns camouflaged the beautiful plants beneath and squirrels, that once thought this was their home, scurried into the distance.

Romin Mukadam (12)
St Martin's School, Northwood

What A Performance!

I stared out of the window, gloomy and annoyed. I was wasting my evening having my face played at and decorated by some mouldy old face paints. I would have to wear a silly, little, humiliating, black bow-tie, which I couldn't even tie up, along with boring school uniform, only to dully recite four sentences.

Rain dribbled down onto the car; not our car, but a friend's car, a friend who had ruined the excuse not to turn up to a play which was to do nothing but bore. It was speedily getting darker, so was my mouth and my temper. The dark silhouettes of trees bounced back, my disposition in an invisible bubble. The street lamps grinned menacingly, spooning light out, casting huge shadows on the sticky, ebony tarmac road.

Daniel Edward (12)
St Martin's School, Northwood

It Wasn't Me!

Oh no, I thought to myself, my heart was beating as if someone was jumping on my heart as if it were a trampoline. Adrenaline was gushing through my body as I wiped my sweaty palms on my rough trousers. *They were here a second ago. Where could they have gone?*

I searched in the interesting, massive science shop that we were all in last, but there was no sign of them. I began to panic and felt very hot. I had ambled through all the shops we had searched, rummaged and run through, but there was no one. I already began to miss my blue teddy that I loved so much. I tried to cool down by drinking all the remains of the heavenly-tasting Coke I had, but I did not. I thought I might save it because that was all I had.

I frantically began to run, trying to find a customer service desk, but I was confused as the giant people ignored me.

Zaid Hamid (11)
St Martin's School, Northwood

The Hanging

The crowds were shaking like a raging bull and the damp, smelly sweat draining the floor made a revolting, sickening smell. Many people quite liked me. You see, I was extremely wealthy; gave it to charity, this made me very popular. Although I lived a double life.

During the long, bright sunny days in London, I was the kind, giving person who was adored by all. However, through the dark, terrifying nights, I was the most fearful gang man of the decade.

None of the crowd wished me to be hanged. The roars of deafening rage were absolutely phenomenal. The only thing I saw was the executioner covered in horrible, rotten, squished tomatoes. The rest I heard through my old, rough ears.

I do not know why the executioners get the nasty blame for murder, because they just earn a normal living and do what they do to survive. The worst sight in this cruel world was openly staring at the condemned. People always feared looking into my eyes because they knew if I did break out, I would murder again. I wouldn't break out, it would never happen. I was one of the most wanted in the revolting streets of London. I was highly secured by the immensely corrupted policemen of the town.

I then got a signal from my gang mates. I was getting out, but not just yet. I perched an evil grin onto my muddy, rough face and slowly blanketed my eyes.

Sachin Hoyle (12)
St Martin's School, Northwood

The View

A stunning view can be seen in Bormio, Italy. The snow shimmering beneath the terracotta sun on the toffee-coloured mountain.

Vanilla snow flecked with emerald leaves and sinister shadows on the snow, caused by beams of light that sit on top of the trees. Smoky, elastic clouds fly by over the mountain. The crystal snow that is covered in gold dots from the glistening sunset, turns a misty night into a beautiful morning.

The graphical, vibrant, volcanic rock gleams in the vermilion sunset, while a thick white blanket of snow covers the mountain. The pear-green trees sit and sway in the morning breeze and a reflection of the trees and mountains can be seen in the dazzling lake, rippling to the beat of the warm summer wind. Soft, silky, dove-white snow sits on the olive green trees, waiting its turn to be blown off the trees by the soft breeze that fills the midday air.

The crystal clear lake twinkles with glory underneath the golden-crusted sun. The lake in Bormio, in the winter sparkles when frozen, but in the summer, eerie reflections of the trees can be seen in the warm lake. The snow-cone mountains look good enough to eat.

Leo Pascoulis (12)
St Martin's School, Northwood

The Woodland

Torrents of light pierced like arrows through the vast canopy of the trees, ejecting dark shadows on the undergrowth below. The wildlife dispersed over an expansive area hidden under the branches. Rustling leaves chattered as the wind compelled them away. Tree branches poked and kicked leaves at one another, childishly. The solid mass of trees brought some relief from rain and acted as a windbreak. There were only small droplets of water that were able to sneak past through the entanglement of trees.

Bugs clustered upon each other and eroded away heaps of mud. Uncivilised. The bark provided a pleasant home with its rough, rigid surface. The moss was growing on the tall trees and it clung tightly. The fungi bulged, tall on the rotting trees, rejected by the sun. The clouds flooded the sky, the sun surrendered under the horizon.

The wind sent flusters of cold air at the shrubs. The smell was the aroma of pollutants. Unclean and littering the air. The swooping birds overhead squawked and poured fear onto the ground. The faint breeze was diluted with a smell of petrol.

A heavy crack, an honest thump, a smash from far away. Then the rest came. Everywhere. Where was I to go? Then it came, blocking my view. I had to make a run. Then I stopped, and I was out of the woodlands as the bulldozer came out too.

James Elliott-Vincent (13)
St Martin's School, Northwood

Flat Number 362

The groaning of the taxi's engine sped off into the distance. Derek looked around - the majestic, dirty flat stood, leaning over to one side. This was Derek's home for the next year and a half. The building was not a particularly exciting one; the paint had flaked off in many places, exposing bare red brick. Water was dripping down from the gaps in the walls; balconies jutted out, complete with rusted rails.

The building was so foul that even the animals seemed to reject it - in fact everybody seemed to reject it - the building was completely empty.

At least the garden was not as bad as the building that accompanied it. The flower beds were shaped in complicated geometrical patterns. These were full of different flowers - golden tulips, red, glossy roses and velvety pansies. These blended together to form a rainbow.

The door of the flat was a grand wooden one, which was clearly in need of some 'tender, loving care'. It creaked when Derek opened it and banged when it was shut. Derek was tired after a long day of travelling. He decided to be lazy and take the elevator. He pressed the button - the old chains hissed as the elevator started groaning into action. Lights indicated at which floor the elevator was. Derek stepped into the lift. A strange creaking sound echoed up the shaft, the lift started rising and finally it reached floor six. Derek had arrived at flat number 362.

Oliver Bello (13)
St Martin's School, Northwood

The Den

I stumbled over the hard ground, trying to follow the narrow path winding its way in and out of the ancient trees. Even the smallest rustle of leaves caused me to turn around wildly, searching for the culprit, but the most I ever saw were the spidery branches of towering trees bearing down upon me, like hundreds of gnarled, twisted hands reaching out into the pitch-blackness of the cool night.

It seemed to take an age to walk to the stream (if you could call it walking), but finally a gentle trickle of water could be heard and the stream swam suddenly into view. I knew that the den was just to the right of the river's bend, so I walked along by the river, keeping my eyes peeled for so much as a hint of danger.

But nothing happened, that is to say, until I reached the river bend and stared into the darkness. Then I saw it. It was well camouflaged underneath an old oak tree. It was made out of countless numbers of dense fir tree branches, all propped up against the trunk of the oak. I scuttled over to it and went inside. It was quite small. The dirt floor was covered in a thick blanket of dry leaves, obviously intended to make the den more comfy and it worked a little, although I would rather have been in my warm bed at home.

Tom Westford (11)
St Martin's School, Northwood

Burning Night

The night had shaken the day into submission and the cold darkness had taken over, grimacing upon what lay beneath. A silhouette lay against the ground, but the figure was hidden amongst the black of the night. The lamp post flickered like man's conflicting emotions. He had been and still was fighting his conscience, but his so-called deed was already done. His vengeance was taking place and the night seemed unchanging. The cobalt neither lightened nor darkened.

A figure lurched proudly out of the darkness and grinned upon the flames dancing, believing it was he who caused all this havoc and destruction. Guilt had flown past and infected someone else's mind. The old, rickety house screamed in anguish as it was being destroyed, and a crash followed its scream. All that was left was silence reflected in the heart of the house.

Vincent Moses (13)
St Martin's School, Northwood

The Lonely Tree

In a field of tobacco dust stood a tree. The tree hung low in its green coat. Rocks, stubborn and solid on the arid landscape, meticulously gazing at the old stump. The clear blue sky danced above them and the sun filtered through the tree's canopy.

The icy dome wept saltwater. Huge puddles surrounded the tree. The grey pebbles, eyes watching him as he rustled the leaves on his arms. Dark shapes crept past and a golden body lay bonded to the tree. The hunters knew that their spoils were there.

Mobeen Syed (12)
St Martin's School, Northwood

Response To The 'Woman In Black'

St Martin's Year 7 and 8 boys went to visit the Fortune Theatre to see the 'Woman in Black' which is a story about an old man telling his terrifying tale. Jenet Humphries is the spooky ghost who terrifies the house. Her face is a skull, it's white and drawn. Her gown camouflages her through the curtains and makes her scarier.

Mr Kipps acts the other characters except for himself because the other actor plays a younger Kipps. Mr Kipps wants to tell his story and he wants to act himself to relive the story. He's the old man that tells his story about how the ghost haunted him and his family. He is a fantastic actor because not only does he change character by changing costume, he changes facial expression and his voice which makes him that character.

The sound effects were the main parts of the play. Every time the mysterious door flung open or the 'ghost woman' appeared, there were loud screams which made me chill. For the first ten minutes try not to fall asleep because the storyline is great.

The props were brilliantly used. They used a hamper for a carriage, desk and a bed. They used an imaginary dog so 'Little Kipps' could talk to someone. There were two actors who made this play a success. It's a must-see play but a bit scary. I would rate it 10/10.

Aramide Oladipo (13)
St Martin's School, Northwood

The Abandoned Cabin

The clay mud path was a pallid smudge up the forest. The grey, hazy drizzle had seldom stopped for the short hour that my boots plodded along this track. On either side were great pine trees, thin slits like soldiers in formation, yet from my view each were scattered all over like stubble on a man's face.

The desolate surroundings swallowed me until I could walk no further. The track had petered out slowly like a firework, brilliant until it stops. As I spun round, the trees that marched along my path were now torn holes in the horizon. All there was was a trampled, grassy trail. My trail was the only hope, so I began to walk. As I ambled through the Welsh woodland, the trail was engulfed by shrubbery and trees. They enclosed every step I took and soon I was isolated. I was lost!

Spinning round blurred my vision. I had lost track of where I'd come from. I silenced as a gust of wind blew up. The forest settled and quietened. Then a beam of light filtered through and as I followed it down I saw a tree shudder. My head jolted round when another tree shivered. I bolted down the thick tree-infested Welsh landscape. The mahogany bark and the emerald treetops fused together as I ran. Rustling of leaves lingered in the back of my mind. I wasn't alone!

Shivum Taank (13)
St Martin's School, Northwood

The Mountain In The Far

I could only hear my own footsteps in the splashing puddles of the olive-green marsh. The segments of rain pelted down through the tiny gaps of the criss-cross branches. The sun took its first glimpse out then over everything else. It towered over the golden bays and the blinding horizon dazzled as the areas of snow soon changed into pale brown rocks. The evil shadows of the trees lapped each other as the warm glowing sun rose, letting out hints of light.

The jagged peak in the distance reflected nicely in the water, its face too vertical to climb. The barriers of the low, misty clouds were too weak to resist the rays of sunlight and the grey clouds began to turn into orange candyfloss that sat in the sky. The mountain's rage grew bigger and bigger as the rough, splashing waves crashed into it.

As the bright yellow, crusted sun rose, the sea started to calm down. Then the gentle waves were pushing up onto the beige sand. I lowered my oar into the lake and disturbed the water, and could see the trickles forming circles in the semi-transparent aqua water.

The little, sweet birds were humming to the falling water. The sparkling water poured down the steep gradient as if it were being pushed over. All around the waterfall on the mountain were the trees and clouds moving in the whistling wind. The trees were old and the rabbits rummaged under the ragged leaves on the ground.

Himesh Naik (12)
St Martin's School, Northwood

The Woods

The heavy rain and floating mist drove out the clear skies. A tiny spark of moonlight was visible, but the glowing flame of the petrol-covered stick was chasing us, being held by one dark, sooty man. We were as scared as we ever would be, shaking as we ran down the sloping hill, but we knew that someone was behind us because we could smell the smoky flames circling the air.

We ran straight ahead into the dark woods thinking that we might lose him. We heard the crackling leaves on the ground being stood on by our heavy, dark black boots. The man was still chasing us, we knew we had to not let the scary-looking man chase us, or we would then be in big trouble.

I tripped over a maroon, cylinder-shaped log. I grazed my shin and the flesh tore inside. The blood was like a tiny, juicy river. Johnny dragged me into a small claustrophobic hole in a tree. The leaves which were the clothes of a tree had been stripped naked which made it like a vulnerable scarecrow. I heard the crackle of the fire on the stick. I knew he was close.

Farhan Zubair (13)
St Martin's School, Northwood

The Woodland And The Tiger

The dark, dry, ginger earth showed only little because of the wild grass and other nature. Sumo wrestlers' waist-sized trees were like umbrellas all that was underneath. Fallen tree trunks' rough barks scratched and drew patterns of nature. To the horizon, bright sun-like rapeseed blossom illuminated the atmosphere while there were patches of daffodils, wild roses, bluebells and buttercups like splashes on an artist's palette.

Birds sat on the trees and sang like a piccolo. Although the green trees' leaves crowded the sky, there were shafts of light. Strong rays of sun, almost blinding, shone on the ground. A little squirrel crept behind another but when it was about to scare the other squirrel, it ran away. Suddenly everything went silent. The wind had stopped, the birds stopped singing and the squirrels stopped chasing.

Il-Kweon Sir (11)
St Martin's School, Northwood

Snow Mountains

At the foot of the mountains there were a few small houses. The houses were blanketed with snow, muffled on the rooftops. They looked like sparkling sugar cubes. The ground was a carpet of velvety snow. The sun was hovering above the mountains, bathing on the trees.

A fresh, but chilly aroma filled the air. The only thing that could be heard was the zephyr sweeping past all land. The trees stood straight and upright like military soldiers. The fiery azure mountains stood, looking like a lump of melted iron, giving a mystical effect. The mountains were covered in a pure white skin of melted snow. Snow lay sprinkled like talcum powder covering the peak.

The scenic beauty of the mountains was magnificent. The sky was a glistening sapphire-blue. The metallic-white snow covered the mountains. The snow was a very pallid white.

Rajiv Kotecha (13)
St Martin's School, Northwood

My Ghastly Garage

My garage is ancient. The doors and windows are covered with dirt and moss like old rags of curtains hanging on. You step inside the damp and soggy building and scattered across the floor are pieces of tiles and mortar fallen from the roof so there are little peepholes of light coming from the ceiling.

There are rolls of gnarled carpet leaning against an antique chest of drawers, but a drawer is missing. Leaning against the cracked and damp wall is my old carpet, it is covered in cobwebs and spiders. Next to my carpet there are my old shoes hanging on rusty nails by thin pieces of faded rope. Next to that is Mum's frail vases, which are just sitting on the floor next to Dad's unused golf clubs, which are either broken or damaged. On the slate-looking walls are shredded maps and you can just make out the countries and seas.

My nose picks up a pungent scent which forces me to leave in a hurry. When I open the door I can see even the sun can smell it because the sun is veiled behind the clouds. I close the door firmly behind me.

Aaron Ashby-Gittins (12)
St Martin's School, Northwood

Newgate Prison

The clank of jail bars closing gave me a shiver up my spine. That sound informed me that I had no hope. The floor was constantly being ambushed by sewer water and rats. The rats had piercing red eyes and fed off dust and dirty sewage water. The whole place had a distinctive damp smell and the only light that came into my cell was a straight beam that came through the peephole windows.

For parts of the day I was chained up to the wall, it made me feel even more hopeless, the cuffs were too tight and the rusty surface of the iron itched my skin. The food was at least five years old, it never changed and it was sloppy.

The cells were packed like an underground station. At 9am, mashed up excretion flowed through my room like water in a river. My feelings were battered, it was as if they were put in a blender. Even if I was in a dump, I made the most of every day. I wondered every day if I would ever see my family again, hopes were low, for I was awaiting my final day.

Krisant Valentine (12)
St Martin's School, Northwood

The Wave Bandits

Like a golden weather balloon, the Caribbean sun presided over the West Indies. Colonel Flute was marching up and down the deck of his twenty-four gun warship, deciding upon a suitable punishment for the men he had found asleep whilst on guard duty.

His second mate, a tall Spaniard with a jungle of black hair and freckles like splashed ink, was in the ship's crow's-nest keeping his large green eyes on the shimmering turquoise ripples of the North Atlantic Ocean.

On the horizon, a group of black dots appeared. From the lookout's eyes they could only have been small fishing boats, but not that far out at sea. With a gasp of shock, the lookout cried, 'Pirates!'

Thomas Minihan (12)
St Martin's School, Northwood

Something To Do

I looked out of the window, watching the garden being smudged like a watercolour painting. It had been raining again. My toy petrol station had water running down the sides. I thought the rain was so selfish not letting me play with it. I heard the click of my dog's paws coming down the corridor. I turned round and saw the ball of fur sniffing under the playroom door. I could smell wet dog. She had been outside. It wasn't fair!

I waddled into the kitchen and I felt warm. The heat seemed to be coming from a giant silver box studded with buttons. I stumbled up to it and then Mummy shouted at me.

'Don't go near that, Reuben.'

Later I found out it was an oven. It seemed fun enough, so I decided to do it for the rest of the day. I plodded backwards and charged at it again. This time Mummy saw me and picked me up and put me outside the kitchen. I sauntered into the kitchen, then out of the corner of my eye I saw something that looked strangely like me. I stared into the oven again. It was another me. It was trapped inside the oven. It had to be freed!

Reuben Green (12)
St Martin's School, Northwood

A Lake

The lake reflects the honey-glazed trees and the blinding, golden, crusted sun, which makes the surface of the lake glisten with a gentle golden glaze.

A cool, refreshing breeze is blowing on the surface of the lake, which is causing tiny ripples to slowly wander from side to side.

There is a small sheltered section of the lake where there is still an icy blanket. It appears to be dazzlingly bright blue and sparkles against the water. There are large dark grey rocks in the middle of the icy blanket. The rocks have a dark green moss over them that seems to match the dark trees that lay behind on the side of the lake. The trees are set in large hills and shaded from the sunlight, except for an area where a ray of light breaks through and enhances the ground.

The lake is wide and the length of it is further than the eye can see. Not too far from the large rocks and ice are small rapids, which are being created by smaller jagged rocks and an old tree that is half collapsed in the location.

In contrast, the other side of the lake is dry and full of beautiful colours made brighter by the sun.

Stephen Kemp (11)
St Martin's School, Northwood

A Perfect Picture

Drenched in golden sunlight, the lush, soft, green grass looked as if it was alive, waving silently in the light breeze, calling you to lie down upon it and sleep. Gardenias and daffodils forced their way up to the sunlight and spread out their leaves into the sky. The sparkling topaz sea was whipped gently by the breeze so it looked like sandpaper. Two dazzling snowy white swans gracefully turned and swam up the course of the sea. The mountains in the distance towered over the lifeless coniferous trees as if to reach out and touch the sky itself. They were encrusted with warm, melting, white snow and were peppered with small boulders so it looked like someone had poured some cream over strawberries. It was like a small amount of icing from a Christmas cake and the black boulders were like the eyes of coal on a snowman.

The mist around the mountains cleared in just a matter of seconds and the fresh, crisp air over the tops of the mountains coloured the sky with a warm ocean-blue. The sky glistened like a sapphire and the clouds were like a puff of smoke floating aimlessly in the air. It was also like a near cloudless sky, soft baby-blue with scattered wisps of cloud. The air was a mixture of different blues. Above the yellow grass, several birds wandered about randomly. Some of them chased each other and glided freely into the air. It was a perfect picture.

Shaneel Shah (11)
St Martin's School, Northwood

Flying Through The Airfield

We stopped running, dead still, fearing whatever lay ahead. Somehow in all the great Armageddon, a silence had blacked out all other sound with the first sight of the man.

'Come here!' I read from the man's lips, yet we had no such thing in mind.

'Quick!' cried Johnny. 'Back, behind the big one - now!'

Johnny grabbed my arm and we were scrabbling away to safety - Johnny again taking the lead. The men had no sight of us with the wall of black smoke hiding us with its thick, wispy, dark velvet vesture.

The man attempted to paddle through the rich river of black but with any possible sight or visibility snatched away viciously from his options, he retreated back to pursue the greater danger - the burning blaze on the other side of the hangar.

Away in another world, separated by the blinding barrier, I crouched behind a bulging body, resting my hands on its smooth surface. The 'big one' was the majestic jet before us, stretching away to our left and right. The plane really was huge when I magnified to this magnitude. Yet the scrubby red line of paint flying across its side did not do justice to the sleeping giant of an engine; silent and hidden away from us inside the plane. There was no time for acknowledgement, the thought of escape was one coated with doubt in my mind and frustration poured out of my mouth.

Breman Rajkumar (13)
St Martin's School, Northwood

The Gloomy Wood

The torch switched on, letting off a brilliant beam of light. I started walking through the patchwork of leaves. Sam dared me to walk into the gloomy wood. A cold shiver ascended my spine. The tall trees towered over me.

I carried on walking, not wanting to see what I was seeing. That was the problem, I couldn't see anything through the dull and pitch-blackness. A thin breeze drifted through the dark leaves. Another cold shiver slowly drifted up my spine. The leaves rustled.

I stopped and looked around. I was looking for something that would give me a clue to where I was going. The paper moon shone through the leaves, giving a kaleidoscope of blackness. I was so scared that my face went as pale as a ghost. Ravens flew through the overturned ink pot of black. I was trapped in ebony. The grass was as cold as ice. The owls hooted. The spiders scuttled down the trees, through the grass and under my feet. The wolves howled to the moon. I couldn't take it anymore. I ran and ran. The torch slipped out of my hand. I ran till my breath was no more. My heart pounded like a drum being hit with the same note. I wished I did not have to do this horrible dare.

I looked for my torch. I tripped on a root bulging out from the ground. I rolled down a steep ditch. The silence was frightened of me. The darkness crept up behind me.

Nikesh Arya (11)
St Martin's School, Northwood

Picturesque Mountains

The butter-yellow sun hung low in the sky. Lazy sugar-coated mountains were illuminated by the bright shining sun. Mountain tops were encrusted with pearl-white snow, which died away into a leafless and lifeless forest. Smooth, delicate fragments of snow, shattered among trees, could be seen under the azure dawn sky.

Ski huts looked like piles of snow, with multicoloured ants walking to and from them. From the incessant chairlift, red, green and blue coloured ants sped past underneath. The secluded mountains had now been found. As time went, the mountain tops would be dented with lines of ski tracks.

In the distance, mountain peaks stood forlornly and the untouched territory was left in peace. Yet far below, a river cascaded down, bobbles of ice like doves standing like paving stones across the river. Then larger brown ants began fishing in the furious river. Minute droplets of ice hung from the tips of their bushy, mahogany coats. Other huge beasts slowly started to come out of the lifeless forest and make their way straight to the river. The timid and shy came out last with their young. About thirty bears were scattered over the stretch of water, all waiting for fish.

As more people flooded in, the slopes were in use. Dawn had gone and the azure sky was glistening all over. The butter-yellow sun shone and as we reached the beginning of the slope, life below had finally begun on the Alps in France.

Paras Shah (12)
St Martin's School, Northwood

An Ancient Castle

I stood before the derelict castle. The cold breeze twirled through my tangled hair. The pallid mist veiled the ancient, crumbly ruin, with towering turrets and steep battlements. A wave of excitement rippled through my body, though on the outside I was anxious. The texture was precise and the wall coarse. A musty odour suffused me whilst cobwebs suspended from the tattered ceiling.

The clouds drifted like ghostly ships calmly through the tranquil sky. I caught a whiff of the eerie silence hovering in the air. Fronds of various plants captured me as I passed. I peered through the shattered window - it was pitch-black. Only the most subtle moonlight passed through via a window. Two tombstones jutted out of the velvety ground, protected by the grave wall, tinted with moss.

I edged closer towards the ruin. My heartbeat grew faster. The jade-green trees swayed slightly due to a subtle breeze. The misted veil of stretched and broken cobwebs hung from the double glazed windows. The mist began to curtain the gravestones as well as the commanding figure of the sagging ruin. I could faintly hear disturbed ornaments chattering on mahogany sideboards. Swirly smoke rose from the desolate castle. A small grey figure was just visible in the deep, damp mist. It was approaching me hastily. I looked back at the ancient castle for the last time and then made my long, tedious journey back home.

Sachin Majithia (13)
St Martin's School, Northwood

Tropical

The aqua sea sparkles and tinkles in the midday sun, interrupted with smudges of olive-green and lime-green. A white boat beautifully skis on the surface of the water, while a handsome yacht streams, ploughing water behind it. The lemon-like sun looms over the mountain. A cloudless tropical blue sky holds three birds, all of them lazily gliding over the sea, also some tiny birds turn and pick at apricots, they turn as if they are clockwork.

A beautiful, pale yellow house is built with terracotta tiles as the roof. If I feel the side I don't feel rough brick but I feel small bumps. Palm trees are stationed around the house, their spiky leaves slice at the house and furry trunk provides a sense of heat.

On the mountain a chunk has been taken off, just like an ice cream spoon curling up some ice cream off the mountain. Up here I can hear a soft whistling sound - that's the wind. Toy-like houses stand on the opposite side, some have square swimming pools and the water ripples effortlessly.

Every single house has a different plant; some olive trees, some orange trees. In one garden a tall palm tree holds tiny mustard-yellow fruits. A lizard snoops around until some children come running towards it shouting, 'Squardo, squardo!' ('Look, look!') The lizard sprints off and hides in a crack while the children look through. An orange cat trots down the road and a red Fiat zooms past, music on high, the cat ignores it.

Patrick Wray (11)
St Martin's School, Northwood

Footsteps From Above

I gripped the torch in my hand. The crumbling house stared at me, looking like the gnarled face of the old woman who'd died in it fifty years ago. The sun shone brightly even though a shadow was cast over the front garden.

'Well, I'm going in. Join me if you don't get scared,' Alan goaded.

Alan was my best friend, even though he had an edge of recklessness I didn't have. He struggled through the creeping weeds to the front door. Alan dared me to go inside the old deserted house, but he ended up going as well.

The silver knocker grinned its gargoyle face at me as we opened the blood-red door and edged inside. Dark shapes danced through the endless shadows. The floor moaned at its new weight, coughing up its dusty throat. A creak answered as the door slammed shut! All I could see was a kaleidoscope of black and grey.

Upstairs something was scuttling.

'Someone's up there,' I whispered.

'Or some thing,' Alan muttered under his breath.

Dark, hollow eyes stared down from a canvas. We had a look around, hoping that something of value was in the house. As we searched without finding anything, our boldness ebbed away like sand in an egg-timer.

In the lounge I found a big chest. Ignoring the fact that the television looked like a fang-filled mouth on legs, I called over to Alan. Freeing the light from the torch's cylindrical cage, we peered inside.

Nicholas Tidmarsh (12)
St Martin's School, Northwood

My Grandma

She has silver-grey hair like thin strands of freshly-woven silk. My grandma has a broad neck which is the trunk of a tree. She wears many gold and silver bangles, embedded with rubies, sapphires and emeralds which makes my grandma glimmer in the midday sun.

My grandma carries a plastic bag with her prized knitting in it and she shows no one until it is finished. The peach sari glows like her warm face. I can just about hear her soft but muffled voice as if she were speaking through a scarf.

My grandma is an extremely competitive person, but kind and passionate. I love my grandma because she just starts gazing into my eyes with her chocolate-brown ones and I start to feel warm inside. As my grandma trundles along, waving her arms briskly, you can smell her Coco Chanel as she passes by. This is my grandma.

Arjun Nijher (12)
St Martin's School, Northwood

Sinbad And The Sirens

Strong waves lashed against the ship. They crashed and roared over the clapping thunder. Rain pelted down and we could hardly see. Lightning flashed. All we could hear was the waves, thunder and shouting. Men fell overboard. The ship got battered against the rocks as I clung to the masts. Or perhaps it would have been better if I had died. Life wasn't as dear to me as it had been. The cacophonous sound of a mast crashing onto the ship erupted. We were going to sink.

Suddenly a beautiful voice started singing. A woman's voice. The chaos around me seemed to become muffled. It was all I could hear. I was enchanted. A beautiful woman glided across the ocean towards me. I couldn't hear anything around me. I couldn't see anything but her, she was transparent and white. She glowed brightly and moved elegantly. She seemed to smile at me while her song still flowed. I didn't know what she was singing but I didn't care.

I reached out for her hand. She reached back. She was walking on water but that didn't seem strange. Her voice stopped and I came to my senses. She had sharp, menacing teeth and cold eyes. Her hands clasped my arm and dragged me overboard. I could hear all the noise around me again. What a fool I was to fall for the siren's trick. Blackness swirled around me, the harsh waters closed around my head. I was drowning.

Abigail Kipps (12)
Waldegrave School for Girls, Twickenham

Little Red's Journey (Told By The Wolf)

I crouched in the bushes surrounding the woods. I had been waiting hours for this meal, if she didn't come soon I would starve.

Just in time! I quickly ducked as she skipped towards me, all smiles. Little Red held a basket and wore her red shawl.

She cautiously crept into the depth of the dark woods. I prowled carefully, making sure I was not seen. Little Red stumbled on some tree roots, silly human. I crouched, ready to pounce on the frightened girl, then remembered my plan and waited. Bending low to avoid the ugly branches, she trudged through the dense trees. I howled in anger, then became furious at my stupidity.

Running ahead, I ducked to hide under the rickety, wooden bridge. She scrambled up, using her two useless legs, then plodded over the top.

I never knew this journey could take so long! She spotted a rabbit and starting stroking it, saying it was cute! When she left I pounced on it, very tasty for a starter.

She was just being annoying. She nearly got lost looking at a perfectly simple signpost! Then, just as she was picking up her pace, she had a sneezing fit, probably hay fever, hate the smell myself, too sickly.

I took this chance. We were approaching the cottage. I growled Little Red shrieked in terror as I leapt; she took out a knife. Yelping, I tried to retreat but the knife struck my throat! I gave one last howl.

Sophie Alys Hopkins (12)
Waldegrave School for Girls, Twickenham

The Handsome Dragon

Once upon a time there lived a lonely dragon called Albert, who led a miserable life in a dark cave in a forest. Albert had no friends so he spent his time sitting in his cave, only going out in the evenings when he would rarely be seen.

One evening, Albert crept out of his cave in search of food. When he was wandering around he met a beautiful princess called Samantha. Samantha was lost and Albert, being a friendly dragon, helped her find her way back home to the palace where she lived. Albert and Samantha became friends and they got on very well. They met every evening in the forest and, after a while, they realised that they loved each other so much that they wanted to get married.

When they announced this to Samantha's parents, the king and queen, they were furious.

'How on earth can you be in love with a scaly old dragon?' bellowed the king.

'But you must look deeper than his skin!' Samantha cried. 'I agree he does *look* beastly from the outside, but if you knew what a wonderful person he is inside, you would love him too.'

The king would not listen and was so outraged that in the night he had his soldiers chain up the dragon so that he could never meet with Samantha again.

Samantha was devastated the next evening when Albert did not turn up for their evening walk. A week went by and Samantha was getting depressed. One evening she walked into the forest much further than she normally went, she couldn't believe Albert would have deserted her. Soon it became dark and she was lost.

'If only Albert were here to help me!' she sobbed.

Just then she saw a cave and decided that she should spend the night there. As she walked in, she saw something chained up in the corner. It was Albert!

Samantha ran over to him and unchained him. She was so outraged with what her father had done that she decided that she would get married to Albert and never return to the palace again. On the wedding day, she kissed Albert and he magically transformed into a young handsome prince and they lived happily ever after in Albert's cave.

Rosie Parr (12)
Waldegrave School for Girls, Twickenham

A Tough Dinner

I'd just lost sight of the squirrel that was going to be dinner that evening. As I stretched I caught sight of a five course meal skipping happily. She was small and skinny, not like the plump boy I'd had for breakfast, but my hunger was so great that nothing would stop me. Slowly and quietly I prowled from tree to tree until finally I was centimetres apart from the girl when suddenly the basket swung around and *bang* right on the head. The girl happily carried on her journey, not knowing what she'd done to poor me. As I managed to scramble back onto my feet, I was able to catch up with her.

The girl, still oblivious to what was going on around her, stopped in her tracks to stroke a rabbit, it was my chance so I slyly crept up behind her and raised my paws, but before my mouth could even open wide enough, she stood up, flinging me back into a thornbush. It was so painful. I never thought I'd put so much effort into getting my dinner, but something about her made me want to carry on.

As she came off the path into the dark gloom of the woods, nothing could stop me - until I saw a shadow lurking behind me, a figure of a man with an axe. *Bash!*

That scar never left me. The angel said I should go and get it checked out. Oh, didn't I tell you? I'm in Heaven now.

Tiffany May Pope (11)
Waldegrave School for Girls, Twickenham

Little Red's Journey

Little Red happily skipped out of her house. She then pranced into the wood. She slipped on a wet leaf which had fallen off the tree, which made her fall to the ground. She soon got back up and wandered on. She later came to a bridge and stumbled over it, but then gracefully pounded down the pebble path. She decided to tiptoe around the sleeping rabbit, so not to wake it up. She started to mutter to herself as she was starting to get bored.

She came to some lovely red apples. She stopped and picked some up, some from the path and some from the grass. She got one for her and one for her gran. She carried on walking, munching as she went. She came to a signpost, she had a quick glance and had to dodge the pretty flowers so not to flatten them.

She bounded on and heard a noise behind her. She stopped, turned and shrieked. There stood a wolf. He pounded to Little Red, but she was clever and got her knife and plunged it in. The wolf went limp and didn't move.

Lauren Yerby (12)
Waldegrave School for Girls, Twickenham

Never Bring Back The Dead

In an old mouldy mansion there was always a little window shining with fire, and facing that window there was also a man, watching and waiting for his late wife to return. Many years later the man stopped waiting and decided to use magic to make his heart whole again, for cancer had taken away a piece from the puzzle in his heart. He walked slowly to the great library and slid his hands through the old dusty books. Luckily his wife was into magic, good and bad. He finally saw the perfect book and read aloud the title - 'Bringing Back The Dead'. He read through carefully so he wouldn't go wrong. He grabbed all the ingredients and was finally ready. The words for the spell were all smudged and he had no idea what they said. He tried his best and read out the spell. A gust of wind flew through the room, opening every door and window, until finally it calmed. White smoke filled the room and then he saw his wife in a ghostly form that shivered his back every time he looked at her.

The next day he could not wait to relive his life again and then suddenly music came from the ballroom. The mansion did not have a CD player and all he heard were violins and gossip and laughter. He ran to the ballroom where he saw a crowd of white people. A huge shiver went down his spine. These were not people, these were ghosts - but not just ordinary ghosts, they were ghosts that had passed away in the mansion he was standing in! He ran back to the book he had read earlier. He tried to make out the words and when he did he wished he'd never seen them, because he hadn't brought back just one ghost, he'd brought back all of them!

As he panicked, an idea suddenly popped into his head. *If there is a spell there must be a reversing spell.* He flicked through the pages as fast as he could and finally found what he was looking for, but there was a problem, one of the ingredients was the feather of a dodo. Of course, everyone knows dodos had become extinct and he had no idea where to get one. Then he thought if there were dead humans there could be dead animals. The search began. He walked slowly into the ballroom and heard screeches of animals, and there it was, the antidote to his *big* problem. He crawled under the crowd, placed his bony hand onto the dodo and was about to pluck.

Across the room there was a huge screech and as he ran as fast as he could to the library he noticed a group of ghosts chasing after him. They didn't want to go! His bony knees shook with fright as he added the last ingredient, said the words, but before he could finish, he had to say goodbye to his wife for the last and final time. The last word came out of him. The same wind whooshed through the room and as he saw the white figures evaporate, he thought that no one else would know about this but him and the ghosts that he would hear in his head every time he entered the ballroom.

Iva Visnjevac (12)
Waldegrave School for Girls, Twickenham

Smash Hits

Juicy Goss

Reggie Yates is a *fraud*. In Fame Acadamy he got *Busted* to sing for him!

McFly Smell

Georgina, 11, has told Tom he smells of the sewers. She lived next door to Tom McFly since she was little and has finally let it out that he stinks!

Celeb Plane Crash

Jamelia, Usher, Akon and Britney were on the same plane flying back to America when the plane broke down and hit the floor. Luckily no one was injured.

Catherine Bell (12)
Waldegrave School for Girls, Twickenham

My Perfect Life
(An extract)

My name is Cresceda. I lived in a children's home by the side of the motorway in Sussex. My life was so dull as I spent most of my time dreaming about being fostered, but I knew that it would never happen as my crappy personality and straggly, twiglet body let me down.

I was beginning to accept who I was and had nearly stopped trying to change my life when one day, whilst clearing the loo, I was called down to see the staff. They said that a couple wanted to see me. I was so flabbergasted and couldn't believe my ears as no one had ever wanted to speak to *me* before. I was hoping that when they saw me they would whisk me away to live in a massive house in New York. That would be fantastic.

Millions of thoughts were running through my mind whilst trudging down the stairs. I hoped they liked me. I reached the office and in there I saw an attractive couple waiting nervously. Their knees were trembling. I walked in, putting on a huge smile and showing off my rotten teeth. I talked to them and I found out their names were Tracy and Kevin and they were rich. They told me I could come and live with them and before I knew it I was moving in with them. It was a dream come true.

Abigail Lyons (11)
Waldegrave School for Girls, Twickenham

Drama Queen
(An extract)

In a village called Wadsworth, there was a girl called Maisie. She was a loving and caring child. She lived with her mum, dad, sister and brother. Her best friends were Megan and Lily and they all loved school, unlike many other children aged nine.

Each day the three girls would walk to school in their navy blue uniforms looking smart and respectable pupils of Wadsworth School, except on Fridays. The three girls disliked Fridays because they did not like their drama lesson at all! They would dread it all week and then it would come on Friday morning, first lesson.

Miss Brown would say in a cheery tone, 'Now we have drama, children, our favourite lesson!'

It was Friday 13th and the time of the day arrived when Miss Brown would say, 'Now we have drama, children, our favourite lesson!' But today she said, 'I'm now going to hand out a copy of the school production and we are going to start to learn our lines! What fun!'

Nooooooo! screamed Maisie in her head.

Each day of the week, Maisie's homework was to carry on learning her lines, but strangely enough she began to enjoy it!

After weeks and weeks of learning her lines, the night had come for Maisie to stand in the spotlight and shine. All the children began to arrive at the school, beaming with excitement. Lots of children came in, practising their parts, but Maisie didn't. Everyone sat in the classroom in their costumes whilst the head teacher said a few words. As it came to the end of Act 1, she walked with Megan to the wing. Then, all of a sudden, Maisie had a mind block and couldn't remember her lines! But it was too late and Maisie had to make her way on to the stage. There was no turning back …

Grace Verghis (11)
Waldegrave School for Girls, Twickenham

Telepinu Goes Missing

My name is Hannahanna and I am the mother goddess. I have one son called Telepinu who is the god of farming. Recently he has become angry with the world, especially polluters. He has run away and no one knows where he is. Weather gods have searched far and wide for him but we have no news. I suggested that we sent a bee to search for Telepinu.

Everyone thought I was mad, but I sent the bee anyway. I mean, just because I am really old doesn't make me stupid.

After about two days, the bee came back and told us that Telepinu was sleeping in the wilderness. My husband was amazed that a bee had found his son.

Kamrusepas, the goddess of magic, asked the doorkeeper to receive Telepinu's anger. There was a loud roll of thunder and lightning. When all this had cleared and I had practically become part deaf, Telepinu returned, riding on the back of an eagle.

Amy Hemsley (11)
Waldegrave School for Girls, Twickenham

A Day In The Life Of A Slave From The Victorian Period

It was freezing in Clara's bedroom. There was no heating, no hot water, not even a proper blanket. All Clara had were her old worn out clothes that were so uncomfortable that they felt like there was an ants' nest in there. Clara had been a slave since she was five. She and her mother had been kidnapped from Africa and were split up. Clara had been through a number of owners, but this family was by far the worst.

Ring, ring, ring, ring. There was the bell to get up. Clara climbed off her mattress with bits of hay sticking out. There was no light in the room so Clara tripped over a couple of things whilst making her way to the stairs. It must have been four in the morning as the church clock was ringing 4am. The head cook was at the top of the stairs, shouting at the top of her voice for everyone to get up.

After cleaning up all the plates from breakfast, Clara now had to make the beds. There were a total of six beds in the house and Clara only had half an hour before she had to do all the washing. Suddenly there was a hush from all the other slaves in the room. Clara turned round to look straight into the mistress' face.

'You, Slave, how much work have you done today?' the mistress bellowed out, looking at Clara with her sharp, narrowing eyes.

'I've done four, My Lady,' Clara stuttered out.

'And what are those chores you have done?'

'Washing the plates, making the beds, making breakfast and taking the younger mistresses and masters to school.' Clara had no idea of what was going on but she was sure it was bad.

The mistress then turned to the head cook and told her to find out who ironed the clothes and put them away as they were to be given ten lashes. Everyone immediately straightened up, trying to smooth out the beds.

Finally it was time for dinner, only Clara would be the last one to have hers, as it was her job to give the owners theirs first. As Clara was walking through the door, Rover, the family's dog, came rushing to her feet. Twisting and turning around her legs, Rover eventually managed to trip Clara over before she could get to the table. Food was everywhere and there were a few broken bowls. Clara was to be given no food and instead ten lashings across her back.

Clara climbed into bed, trying not to lie on her back. The pain was like there were lions trying to attack her and every second a claw would dig into her back. Clara cried herself to sleep, knowing that the next day would be the same as it always had been.

Catherine Ollington (12)
Waldegrave School for Girls, Twickenham

A Day In The Life Of A Child In World War II
(An extract)

Our house in Teddington was quiet. Yesterday we had pottered in our vegetable patch and Dad had done the finishing touches to our air raid shelter. He put a small shelf and our old fridge in there in case we got hungry or we were in there for a while. Our new ration book and our favourite belongings are kept inside the air raid shelter. The shelter is like many others, covered with sand bags and big enough for Mum, Dad, James, Grandma and I all to fit in.

Today is the 17th of September 1939, 4 days after my twelfth birthday. Mum was hanging out the washing at the time. Dad had just finished his training, as Dad is going to be a warden, and Grandma was darning the socks. I was playing on the street with my next-door neighbour, Lucinda, and I could see my little brother, James, playing ball in the distance. Suddenly I heard the sound I had been dreading. It was the first time I'd heard it, but I knew what it was. It was the first air raid siren of the war. The Germans were coming!

There was so much confusion. All around me, people were screaming. All I could think about was to get into the air raid shelter. I ran into the house, found that Mum, Dad and Grandma were in the shelter. I ran in there, just in time. The first bomb had gone off not too far away. One down, one million to go.

I took a deep breath as I turned around to look at Mum. Her eyes were full of fear. I held her hand tight and just at that moment I knew I had lost something. 'Where is James?' I asked Mum, she didn't know, she thought he was with me. Dad started to panic as bomb after bomb went off. Each time I thought of James. *Where could he be?* He must have a bit of common sense; he had had war safety lessons at school just like me. Mum was crying at this point. I think I was too. All we could do now was hope, pray and wait.

Emilie Ruddick (12)
Waldegrave School for Girls, Twickenham

Little Red's Journey

Little Red grabbed the basket her mum gave to her and skipped out the front door. She then swung the gate closed and began to skip into the huge, dark forest. It was gloomy and the trees swayed from side to side. It seemed as if they were going to pounce on her. Little Red, determined to carry on, tiptoed on through the forest. The forest trees were old and wrinkled, and it was almost as if the rubbing trees were whispering amongst themselves. Little Red then slowed down, not noticing a wolf creeping up behind. The sly wolf snuck behind, making sure she couldn't see him. He desired her. He licked his lips and dribbled all over the floor.

Soon, Little Red came out of the dark forest and felt relieved but then she stumbled over a really rocky bridge. She then looked behind and suddenly a rabbit pounced on her. She screamed, then stopped. The rabbit immediately hopped away, really frightened. Little Red felt silly and laughed.

While screaming, she had dropped the apples, so she decided to sit down and eat one as she was hungry. As she was eating, the sly wolf was still lurching behind. He watched her like a hawk. Little Red jumped up and began to walk again. She then came to some flowers and tripped over a rock! Then she heard a creepy howl. She got up and began to run.

Henna Lakha (12)
Waldegrave School for Girls, Twickenham

No One Knew Him

It was very dark in the old village of Glass-May and there was a boy who nobody knew.

Sophie was 11 years old and very well-behaved. She lived in Glass-May with her mum. Sophie never knew her dad because he divorced her mum when Sophie was little. There were only a few houses in Glass-May and one of them was the biggest of them all, Glass-May Castle. Sophie had always wondered who lived in that dusty old castle.

Sophie lived in the house opposite the castle. Sophie's house was neither big nor small. Her house was beautiful with little windows and little white and red curtains. Sophie went to a local school in the village. She knew everyone except the boy in the corner. No one knew who he was or where he lived.

One day, Sophie decided to go and talk to the boy who always stayed in the corner. As soon as Sophie said hello the boy looked at her with gleaming eyes. They were so bright that they looked like car headlights.

Sophie paused and then said, 'So ... um ... who are you?'

'I'm Timmy Longstun.'

'Well, I'm Sophie and I'm pleased to meet you.'

'So am I,' said Timmy. 'Sorry, it's just that no one's been talking to me since the day I came to this school and sometimes I feel as though I'm invisible.'

'Oh, I'm sorry,' said Sophie. 'Whereabouts do you live then?'

Timmy stopped and said, 'Um ... I ... live ... in ... Glass-May ... Castle.'

Sophie was not surprised or shocked. She just stood there with her beautiful smile.

The next day Timmy asked Sophie if she would like to go to his house. She agreed. When it was the end of school, they both walked home together. Timmy opened the gates and they went in. From that day forward, Timmy and Sophie were best friends.

Amy Barnett (12)
Waldegrave School for Girls, Twickenham

The Salem Witch Trials - The Deception
(An extract)

'There is no happy ending without slight complication' -
David Eddings.

The day had been harsh, I was weary and tired from riding out to fetch berries. The air was cold, and yet, the wind was dead and the trees gnarled with age. There was a deathly silence in the air as my cloak and hair veiled my horse's back. Salem had lately been bewitched. They said that the Devil had arrived and tainted the people in our villages. When one girl started screaming, all three of the Willis' young ladies had burst out, causing an uproar.

The days were darker in summer and little joy in the Applegate Inn. Men stopped singing, lovers stopped kissing, even children stopped crying. It was as if the village, the gates, the people, the gallows and the law house were all holding their breath. Liars stalked the streets, pretending to be bewitched, I say this as I do not believe there is real witchcraft at hand.

Forgive me, I must introduce myself. I am Lekka Neels, wife of Hal Neels, mother of Cristophe Neels. The women at the inn call me 'Wise Owl' because I sort problems and am fond of the creatures named 'owls'. Despite being young, I am one of the brightest people in the village, so I was supposedly the best at running the Applegate Inn.

The stony silence at the inn was unbearable. Cold weather was starting to stab at the slight warmth, with the warning that autumn was nearly nigh. The last man, Jerry Higgins, exited the inn as it turned midnight and I started to think about going to bed as no more customers, no matter how inebriated, would ever stay out after the last strike of midnight. Just thinking of him, my husband entered the door.

He said, 'Another person has been trialed.'

I asked, 'Sentence?'

And words I did not wish to hear, 'Death.'

We went to bed with frowns on our faces and a mix of grief, yet grimness in our hearts.

Stephanie Marquardt (11)
Waldegrave School for Girls, Twickenham

Wolf

It was a dark night and all the wolf could hear were birds squawking, owls hooting and the never-ending knock of the woodpecker. The wolf was hungry and he was craving for a bite from juicy flesh, which is why he always kept watch of the path in case something might come skipping by, or in other words, right into the wolf's mouth.

Then one bright, sunny day, a little, juicy, yummy, fresh little girl was on the path. Prowling under the undergrowth, the wolf pounced, knocked the little girl's cape off and he saw her running off.

The wolf was disappointed with his foolishness, he should have waited until her tiredness had overcome her and that meant she would sit down, but to the wolf he had already messed it up. Suddenly, after a few minutes, to the wolf's disbelief, she had come off the path.

'Well, my luck is in after all and what a prize she is,' the wolf said, cackling to himself but the thing was, the wolf was faster than the little girl. He used his speed so he could surprise her at her grandmother's house.

It was about an hour later when the wolf had swallowed Grandmother, when the little girl had come.

She came inside, saying, 'Morning Grandmother.'

The wolf replied with a most high-pitched tone, 'My dear, would you mind coming here for a sec, I am hungry.'

She came and that was the end of her.

Imogen Mathews (12)
Waldegrave School for Girls, Twickenham

The Big, Dark Woods

Once there lived a big girl who lived in a big house with her big mum, her big dad and her big family. They all lived happily in the big woods in the middle of the big world. One day big Lisa was walking the big dog in the big woods until she came upon a big castle and stopped!

She was amazed at the size of the big castle, so decided that she would take a big wander in the big castle. As she approached the big door that led into the big castle she saw a big note with big writing on it saying that no kids could enter the castle. She had a big grin across her big face, thinking that she should go and explore the big castle.

She opened the big door and there was a big guard. She crept past the guard and went into a big room, where she wandered further into the room. She realised a big king on a big chair had spotted her, so she turned away and started running. He had caught up with her. She turned around and he was closer but then to her *big* amazement, she tripped and that was the last time we saw big Lisa!

Taylor Rowe (12)
Waldegrave School for Girls, Twickenham

A Day In The Life Of Happy The Clown

I was the happiest clown ever to perform on stage, but when I was backstage I was the most miserable clown in the whole world. The big lights, the massive shoes and the funny faces were just not right for me.

I had to run out onto the stage endlessly and be as happy and as funny as I could whilst the crowd clapped and cheered. But inside, I felt miserable, annoyed and lonely all at the same time.

It used to take me hours to put that huge, red smile on my face. I hated it so much, but it covered up my sad face and that was the main thing. I never had many friends at the circus, unless you could say that people calling you horrible names and throwing eggs at you were being nice.

I remember one night when I came on stage doing my impressions and it suddenly hit me. Why not leave the circus? I quickly finished my performance, packed my bags and sprinted out of the circus. I think I lasted about a night before crawling back to the circus.

But at least that taught me a lesson. You don't know what you've really got until you lose it. And I never left the circus again.

Hattie Morgan (12)
Waldegrave School for Girls, Twickenham

Life Is Not That Boring

Once upon a time a little girl called Cameron always wished she would find her prince charming. She was always the odd one out and wanted to be noticed. She never fitted in and as much as she did love her family, they treated her differently from her sister and brother. She always wanted to be the popular kid, but never was.

She set off one day to explore life as if there was not much time left. She didn't tell her loving, caring family that she was going and just left a note saying she had gone and was going to be happy in a different lifestyle. Cameron got on a bus to the airport where she was going to fly to New York! All her luggage was on board and then her flight was ready to fly off to another world of adventure and exciting new beginnings to find and treasure for life. She received a call from her mum and dad; they were worried sick and missed their little girl. Cameron said nothing and cut off the line.

Later on, her father called the police and got them searching for their little girl, only 14 years old, would be 15 next month. Her daddy got loads and loads of police to search but still nothing.

Later on the aeroplane, she met a guy called Justin Timberlake. They chatted for hours on end. She liked him and thought he was gorgeous. It was as if she had disappeared from her old stinky life to her new, fantastic, amazing world which was brilliant. Justin asked if he could see her again, so they arranged a date and met up at a club. What Cameron didn't know was that he was a singer and had dedicated the song to her. They were friends for years and when Cameron was 21 she started going out with him, but then it got complicated as she hadn't spoken with her parents for years when suddenly they rang her. Cameron answered her phone and there were her parents speaking on the other end! She didn't know what to say or do. They asked her to come home and have her old life back. She cut off and sat grumpily on her wide sofa.

She didn't know what to do and asked Justin who was now a singer and one of the greatest. What she didn't know was that Justin was going to ask her to get married to him. It was that night he performed and he sang a song for her and in that song he asked her to marry him! She shouted, 'Yes!' They got married and Cameron sorted out everything with her parents. They all lived happily ever after …

Katie Zgorska (12)
Waldegrave School for Girls, Twickenham

The Day I Walked In

It was a dark, cold night when I heard a noise. I was in shock. It started to rain. I saw a hotel so I walked in and left the door open behind me.

Suddenly it closed. I tried to open it but I couldn't. I was terrified. I shouted for my mum but all I could hear was my echo. I started to wander round the hotel and I came to a block of stairs.

I walked up the stairs. I was so shocked, it was like the stairs never ended, so I didn't bother. I came downstairs with aching feet and I saw this book so I wrote in it. I wrote, 'Somebody help me'.

After a while it faded away and a message came up saying, 'Who are you?' I was so terrified that I closed the book quickly. I looked at the time, it was 10pm and I was tired so I went upstairs to find a bed to sleep on.

I woke up at 9.30am and I went downstairs and tried to open the door. It opened. I screamed, 'Yippee!' It was like yesterday never happened, so I walked out the door and I ran home.

The next thing I remembered was that I was late for school. I shouted, 'Oh no, please say this is not happening.' When I went to school I had a detention.

Aziza Khanom (12)
Waldegrave School for Girls, Twickenham

Child In The Road

Jenny was on her way to work and was driving down Hampton Hill High Street. She worked at Waldegrave, a secondary school in Twickenham. Suddenly she saw a child run out into the road after a ball. She slammed on her brakes but did not stop in time and hit the child.

Everyone behind her was beeping. She slowly got out of the car but there was nobody on the road. She got back in her car and continued to drive to work. She did not know what had happened, maybe it was a ghost, maybe she'd imagined it.

The next day when she was going to work she saw the same child running out in front of her car. She slammed on her brakes and heard a loud smash. The person behind her had crashed into her, but when she went to look for the child on the road, no one was there. This kept on happening for a week and Jenny began to get scared.

She went to see her doctor. He said that she must have been imagining it and told her to go a different way. She went a different way for about another month, but one day she slept in and was very late for work so she went down the high street. She was about 20 metres away from the place where the child normally ran out.

She saw the child running out and thought it was her imagination. Instead of hitting the brakes, she hit the accelerator and sped up. Suddenly she heard a bang on her car. She stopped and got out. She looked in front of the car and saw a child dead in the road!

Suzie Harrison (12)
Waldegrave School for Girls, Twickenham

The Magician

I never expected our move to England would involve such an exciting adventure. It all started at my birthday party. Having just moved here from Australia, I didn't know many people. I decided to invite my two closest friends for a sleepover at my house.

My parents bought our house very cheaply. We didn't know why we got such a bargain, but people said it was because it was haunted. We didn't believe them, after all, neither did our neighbours.

Once my friends arrived for my party we all went into my room and got into our pyjamas. We were just talking about the latest films we had seen when Amy suddenly spoke.

'How about we explore your house tonight? We can get everything ready, go and eat dinner like nothing's happening and then, when it's bedtime, we can go!'

We all agreed and set off around the house searching for bits and bobs we might need. Afterwards, we all came to the kitchen for our delicious dinner of pesto pizza and salad. We all chatted for ages and then got ready for bed. So far the plan was working!

Once my mum put us to bed we retrieved the bits and bobs from under my bed and then we all waited for the all-clear sign. I had a really small trapdoor in my room which looked like a very small cupboard, so that's where we started the journey. We were crawling through a dirty tunnel for what seemed like ages until Katy suddenly stopped.

'Ellie, there's a door, what should I do?' asked Katy.

'Go in, obviously,' I replied. 'What else are we going to do? We can't turn back now!'

We all squeezed through the door into a room I had never been into before.

'Where are we?' asked Amy, confused.

'I don't know but I'm going to find out!' I said determinedly.

Then we heard something. Clanking chains, a little boy shouting, 'Help!' People laughing. We all screamed. I ran out of the room, followed by Katy and Amy. We squeezed back through the door, through the long corridor, out of the trapdoor and into the living room.

Then we all burst out laughing. My next-door neighbours have a little boy who likes to do magic tricks. He must have been doing his famous chain trick because he was all tied up, wriggling around, and shouting for help. The laughing was coming from his parents who were watching him.

I never forgot that night, but it taught me one important thing: don't let strange noises in the night scare you; it's probably just your neighbours.

Ilana Blum (11)
Waldegrave School for Girls, Twickenham

A Day In The Life Of A Famous Person

I woke up in the morning in my four storey mansion, knowing that it was going to be another hard day, running away from the paparazzi. It's always the same, whatever you do, wherever you go, the paparazzi are always there, shoving cameras in your face. You can't even go into your garden without being watched over the fence by a guy with a big, flashy camera!

Today I had decided I would go shopping in town. I got dressed into some baggy jeans and a T-shirt, had breakfast and walked out the door. As usual there was that freaky guy hiding behind the hedge who thought I couldn't see him! I got into my red Audi TT and set off into town.

I parked my car and started walking to the nearest shoe shop when three young girls stopped me.

'Please. Please can we have your autograph?' one of them pleaded.

'I can't believe I've actually met you!' the other said.

'Of course you can have my autograph!' I said in a false happy voice. What else could I have done? I couldn't really say no to a couple of young teenagers could I?

I signed their papers and continued on down the busy high street. Everyone was staring and pointing at me. I entered my favourite shoe shop and bought a new pair of stilettos. I could see tomorrow's glossy magazine headlines: 'Famous Person Buys New Pair Of Stilettos!' I couldn't see why everyone thought it was so interesting!

After about three hours of shopping I headed home. The freaky paparazzi guy had given up and had headed home too. I got inside, dropped my bags and flopped onto my sofa. I sat there and started to think. Everyone wants to be famous, but I would be just as happy being normal like everyone else. Being famous isn't all what it seems!

Sophie Wilson (12)
Waldegrave School for Girls, Twickenham

Little Red

Little Red waved goodbye to her mother as she skipped among the crisp autumn leaves, away from the comforts of her home. She soon came to a long, dark wood where all the trees towered above her. As she crept through the wood she could hear the multicoloured leaves swirling around and the faint, distant cry of a wolf.

It wasn't long before she came to a rickety bridge. The innocent little girl trundled across the bridge unaware that she was being watched by the beady eyes of a drooling wolf. It was getting colder so she decided to wrap her cloak around her. She was dreaming about her mother who was selling apple cider at the local market so she could give Little Red a good education.

As she dreamily glanced ahead, she saw a sweet little bunny rabbit and tiptoed over to stroke it. The rabbit darted away as Little Red's tummy made a loud rumbling sound. She saw an apple tree and picked a few apples off the low branches of the small tree. She was still happily munching when she saw a patch of flowers. She used her father's hunting knife to slice a few off for her grandmother.

She was still clutching the knife when the wolf made a sly pounce for her. Little Red swerved round and swiped off the sly wolf's head. The dead body dropped on the floor. Little Red drifted off into the distance.

Sashka Young (12)
Waldegrave School for Girls, Twickenham

Life Lost

I know you may think this will be one of those stories with tragic loss of life, but this is menacing. I'm Jess, the girl out on her own with courage but no hope. I'm still here in the shadowy place where it all happened. But everyone reassures me this didn't happen.

I first got that horrible call two weeks ago, which you know will happen one day, but you don't want it to.

'Your mother died.'

I cried hard, making a puddle of a thousand tears. It was like having my heart smashed to pieces and no glue. Then there's the will.

'Your mother's haunted house.'

I decided to go and sleep there as one last chance to remember my mother and prove everyone wrong. I stayed there in that creepy room with dust hanging from the ceilings, my mother's bedroom. I did not stay up long, as looking round the house broke my heart. I drifted off to sleep.

Suddenly a flashing light shone in front of me, getting bigger and brighter as I walked towards it. It had a pale face, hair like a mop, worn out. The ghost then spoke. It was my mother. I froze. I stood there staring, wondering what to do. Was this a dream or reality?

I talked to her, my face lit up as I knew she was still here. Smiling, I blinked. She was gone.

I sit here, telling you, as if you have lost one, there is always hope.

Catherine Hale (12)
Waldegrave School for Girls, Twickenham

When It Happened

I write this now on the scrap of paper I found. If somebody reads it I'll be put in jail. I suppose it's better than this place. It all started 10 years back ...
    I was 17 and at college. It was nearly the day of my birthday. I decided to go to the seaside. I said to my friends, 'Why don't we go to the seaside?'
    We went the next day. I looked at Sarah. I hated her, why did she have to come along?
    When we got there we sat down on the sand. I said I was going to walk to the cliffs.
    'I'll come with you,' replied Sarah.
    I nodded. Before we knew it we were up on the cliffs. Sarah was really getting on my nerves by now as she was talking about me and my behavioural problems.
    'What's your problem?' I shouted at her. I remember her innocent face. I was angry with her. I hate anyone who speaks of my problems. I grabbed hold of her. 'I asked you a question,' I shouted, spitting at her.
    She didn't answer. She was frustrating me. I couldn't control myself, and that's when I did it. I threw her over the side of the cliffs. That one moment that brought me where I am now. That one moment that changed my life ...
    Now I'm here in this mental home. I thought they'd believe my story. Now they won't believe the truth. If only ...

Neetu Dhillon (12)
Waldegrave School for Girls, Twickenham

Portal Box

Millions of years ago, way before any recording of any life had been discovered, there was the most advanced civilisation that anyone had ever known of.

My full name is Katherine Mary Mason. I awoke by the rattling noise of a hover car whizzing outside the window. Then there was the sensation of realising that it was the first day of the summer holidays. I dragged myself out of bed and slipped on some clothes. I picked up a breakfast smoothie, my favourite, bacon, eggs and hash browns with ketchup. I pulled out of the garage and unfolded my motorbike. I then swerved into the road tunnel. It is completely simple my bike, you don't even have to control it, you just tell it where to go and you're there.

I set off to the park. I decided to go down a different path. It was overgrown and seemed like it had never ever been touched before. I set off, it was bumpy, dark, spooky and gloomy. It was so fun, exciting and adventurous. Just then I leapt off my bike over the handlebars and into a pile of ivy. My leg throbbed with pain so I decided to take my mind off my injury by scrambling around to see what I had hit. It was a strange box covered in dirt. I opened it and there was a blinding light. I landed in a world unlike my own, a world that was quite modern to everyone else around me. It was the year 2005.

Francesca Twynam (11)
Waldegrave School for Girls, Twickenham

One Cold Day!

It was a 'shiver up your spine' day. Gracie, a normal 13-year-old, left home, Jasmine Cottage, to do her dad's postman job as he was poorly.

An ordinary, blustery day you might think; so did Gracie, but you are far from right, this was the worst day Gracie had ever had.

As Gracie ambled along the village path, she came to a house she had never noticed before. She continued delivering letters, but heading home, she realised that there was one letter still in her shabby bag. It read: *150 Manor Lane, Small Town*. 'What house could this be?' she thought aloud. But then she remembered, 'That old house I went past.' So she returned to the house.

Gracie was a timid sort, but her curiosity got the better of her with this dilapidated house. It seemed that someone was expecting her as a key was in the lock. Gracie turned it and tugged at the battered door.

'Come in,' cackled a low voice from behind her.

Before she could look, the person whipped her down by her dishevelled hair. She screamed! Then she realised no one could hear her.

'I have been waiting for you, Jim,' a man said.

'I'm not Jim,' she cried. 'Help!'

'I have only ever felt bitterness to your family,' the man laughed. The man pulled out something sharp and shiny. A dagger!

No one ever saw Gracie again. Her mother sobbed throughout the memorial service. The mystery was never solved, until today!

Rachel Budden (12)
Waldegrave School for Girls, Twickenham

The Message Beneath

It felt like I couldn't breathe. I was out of control. The iPod, the power had overtaken my brain. I couldn't think. I didn't know what to do. Was I going to die because of this? Then it did it again, the iPod flashed with another message.

'I know what you want and I have it, don't tell anyone or you know what is going to happen'.

Do I know what is going to happen? No I don't and what could happen? It is not like it is controlling my brain is it?

Suddenly my legs started to shake and ... I began to run, but why?

Then the message came again. 'Don't look behind you or you will experience a very slow and painful death in Hell!'

This shocked me, but I daren't look behind me. What was I to do? My brain was swimming and searching for thoughts, but none came to me.

Why would a person do whatever it is they are doing? After thinking, I got very tired and I was constantly yawning.

I must have fallen asleep because when I woke up I was at my desk in university in the middle of a psychology lesson!

Suddenly Mr Watkins said, 'Sometimes the brain can see things that aren't true, so the brain makes up a whole new story. Sometimes they are married or have children but this is all not true, so we are ...'

I stopped listening to him when I thought ... *so brains can make up a whole other world that never happened but they think it did. I wonder if that is what happened to me?* I looked down and I saw my iPod next to me.

The message on the front said, 'You might have killed me but the message lies beneath'.

Jessica Wolf (11)
Waldegrave School for Girls, Twickenham